NAVAT

CONQUERED WORLD: BOOK SEVENTEEN

ELIN WYN

CLOCK
WALK
PUBLISHING

NAVAT

"You know what angers me?" I grumbled as I stalked down the corridors.

"What?" Sakev asked me.

"I've done this before. The humans have a phrase for it. Experiencing the same moment over and over again?"

"Déjà vu," a voice piped up from behind me. I looked over my shoulder to see Amira, a spunky human and the sister-in-law of Strike Team One's leader, Vrehx. Since Jeneva gave birth, she'd taken a step back from her duties in General Rouhr's organization. I supposed Amira had picked up some of the slack in her sister's place, though I hadn't talked to her much.

She seemed okay. Tough as nails and determined as skrell. Then again, all the humans had to be tough as nails now, even the gentle ones like Dr. Parr. Their planet- our planet now- couldn't seem to catch a break.

"Déjà vu," I repeated, testing the strange syllabus on my tongue.

"It means *already seen* in French, one of the old Terran dialects" Amira explained. "You literally feel like you've already seen and done this before."

"That's exactly it," I muttered. "And it pisses me off."

"Elaborate," Sakev jerked his chin in my direction.

"Remember that whole deal with the Xathi hybrids?" I said. "I feel like I've already gone through the human population and cleansed it of an invasive species. I'm not thrilled about having to do this all over again. What was the point of doing it all the first time if we're right back where we started?"

"It's not exactly the same," Amira offered. "For one thing, the hybridism antidote we concocted does jack shit for this new type of possession. Xathi hybridism operated like a plague, a virus. This is a brain thing. A weird brain thing."

"Is that the technical term?" I smirked.

"Shut up," Amira chuckled. "This isn't my field of expertise. I'm learning as I go, just like everyone else here."

"Fair enough," I shrugged. "Do you ever get sick of all this?"

"Of course," she scoffed. "You think I want to be

dealing with Xathi, Puppet Masters, and whatever this new fresh hell is?"

"Gorgoxians," Sakev said. "The anti-alien dickheads are calling them Gorgos for short. I hate those fuckers but it's catchy."

"Which fuckers?" I asked. "The anti-alien dickheads or the Gorgos?"

"Both."

"I second that," Amira quipped. "The last year has been one never-ending migraine."

"Even the part where you fell in love?" Sakev teased.

"Especially the part where I fell in love," Amira winked. "Speaking of love, Dax said he'll be along to help out shortly. He's in a meeting right now."

"Do you think we'll need him?" I wondered. "Sakev and I have more than enough muscle between the two of us."

"Theoretically, we won't need him," Amira explained. "However, when have things ever gone according to theory for us?"

"I think it happened once a few weeks ago," I joked. "But seriously, any idea what we're dealing with today?"

"The scouting group hasn't checked in yet," she said.

"Isn't that concerning?"

"I'm choosing to believe no news is good news." The nervous glint in her eyes didn't escape my notice.

"When has that ever been the case for us?" I asked, instantly regretting my words.

"Never," Amira admitted. "But anything is possible, right? This past year has surely proved that."

"Without a doubt," Sakev agreed.

We've reached one of the newly renovated holding cells. It'd been reinforced five times over since it was redone. Right now, it stood empty.

"Now what?"

"Now we play the waiting game," Amira sighed. "I'll try to get the scout team on the radio."

"Be cautious," Sakev warned. "If they're closing in on a target, a radio call might give away their position."

"Good point," Amira tapped her chin. "I'll try to get their navigation location on a datapad."

Amira walked off in search of a datapad. I turned to Sakev.

"I'm still pissed off."

"When are you not?" Sakev joked.

"I've been pissed off since I joined the Valorni ranks," I said.

"Trust me, I'm aware," Sakev laughed. "Do you regret it, though?"

"I don't think so," I said after a moment of consideration. "I mean, we've landed in a shit situation here. I know not everyone thinks so, especially the lucky ones who found mates," I gave Sakev a pointed look. He grinned back at me.

"You jealous?" He asked.

"Not exactly," I shrugged. "I'm jealous that some have found reasons to make staying here worthwhile. I don't need a mate thrown into this mess, though. It'll only complicate things."

"Let me put it this way, what would you be doing if you weren't here?"

"Probably doing the same thing somewhere else," I laughed dryly. "The Xathi are still wreaking havoc elsewhere in the galaxies. Odds are, I'd be doing the same thing I'm doing now only without the support of Strike Teams and a good General. I wouldn't be a civilian."

"There you go." Sakev clapped his hands together. "You're not pissed about being a soldier. You're just pissed off. It's part of your personality."

I laughed genuinely this time.

"Thanks for the pep talk. You should start charging for them."

"I know, right?"

"I got something!" Amira rushed into the room, datapad in hand. "The scout team is heading back."

"Did they get a Gorgo?"

"I think so," she replied. "And we shouldn't call them that. They're still people."

"They're husks," I said flatly. "The Gorgo is the one steering the ship if you catch my meaning."

"Still, it skeeves me out," Amira shuddered. "They're people. When the new subject arrives, we should treat them as such."

"Only if they act as such," I said decisively.

"You're an asshole, Navat. Has anyone ever told you that?" Amira grinned.

"Many times," I smirked. "What kind of prep do we need to do for our new guest? Food and water bowls?"

"Please, never reproduce," Amira jabbed.

"I have great paternal instincts, for your information," I shot back.

"I'll believe that when I see it. Get ready. The scout team is back."

Amira grabbed the radio from Sakev's belt and clicked to the correct frequency.

"Talk to me. What do we have?"

"Single subject," a staticky voice came through. "Displaying no signs of aggression. Minimal signs of awareness."

"You're sure it's an occupied host?" She asked, wincing on the words.

That was the tricky thing about the Gorgos. They tended to overload their hosts. We'd noticed they've gotten better at abandoning a host before a host dies, but that wasn't a good thing. Vacated hosts were... screwy, for lack of better word.

So far, the vacated hosts we'd observed were nothing like they were before the Gorgo invaded their minds. Best case scenario, it was like they were drugged or in some kind of haze. Worst case was a host gone mad. We hadn't found a way to reverse that yet. The ladies up in the labs were working on it night and day but they had almost nothing to work off of.

Enter the scouts.

We'd all had a turn on the scout teams but some were a better fit than others. I was better suited to the second phase: dealing with the subject.

Now that Einhiv was basically a Gorgo colony, the scouts had a good hunting ground to pick up affected humans.

The front doors to the holding facility were kicked open and a small group of heavily armored scouts entered the room. Each had a hold on a human woman who looked far too pale for comfort. There was a telltale glazed look in her eyes. She wouldn't even move her feet. They were dragging behind her. I could see that the scouts were doing whatever they could not to injure her in the transport process but she didn't seem aware of what was happening around her.

She didn't put up a fight as she was put in the

holding cell. Two scouts gently placed her in a chair before taking their leave.

"She's all yours," one of the scouts, a human male, nodded to us. We didn't have many human volunteers. It was nice to see one on our side.

"Thanks," Amira nodded back. She looked at the woman in the holding cell. "Can you tell us your name?"

The woman said nothing. She didn't even blink.

"We're going to run a few tests on you," Amira explained. "They aren't supposed to hurt so if you feel any pain, you need to let me know immediately. Can you do that?"

No response.

"Can we even test on her like this?" I asked.

"We don't have a choice. Every ounce of information we can get is helpful."

"But will she be able to tell us if something is wrong?"

"I'm not sure," Amira frowned.

"That's some kind of ethical violation isn't it?" Sakev wondered out loud.

"We're ethically obligated to protect the women, but not the Gorgo. If the Gorgo is present inside her, we're obligated to test on it."

"I understand what you mean about those migraines, Amira," I groaned.

With the anti-alien presence still strong in most of the cities, General Rouhr and Mayor Vidia wanted us to take extra precautions with everything we did. The last thing we needed was to be accused of treating people inhumanely.

After everything we've done to keep the human population safe, it was ridiculous that we still didn't have their full trust.

Leena breezed in, scrolling through her notes. Dr. Parr followed closely behind.

"Are we ready to start testing?"

"I can't verify the presence of a Gorgo," Amira said.

"We'll start with the gentlest test first," Leena decided. "She shouldn't feel a thing. Gorgo or no Gorgo."

"Works for me," Amira shrugged.

The reinforced walls and windows in the holding cell weren't the only renovations. This cell, in particular, was set up for testing. All of the scanners and other fancy technical stuff was already installed. Leena could run tests without going into the holding cell.

"Running test one: Thermo scan," Leena spoke into a recorder. She pressed a few buttons on her datapad.

We'd figured out that Gorgo's affected the body temperature of the host. An occupied human's temperature ran over one hundred degrees.

Machinery whirled. All of our eyes were fixed on the woman. She still hadn't reacted to anything around her.

Once the thermal scanner fired up, that all changed.

She went ballistic. She screamed and thrashed, leaping out of her seat to slam herself into the reinforced walls which, thankfully, held.

"Should we turn it off?" Amira asked.

"No." Leena's gaze went steely. "This is a new reaction. We have to observe."

"She's going to break her face," I said.

"We can release tranq gas if it gets too serious," Leena said. "Dr. Parr is here for a reason, as well."

The woman turned to us. It was difficult to explain, but it looked as if there was a second face beneath her actual face.

The Gorgo.

The woman let out a howl. The second face disappeared. She collapsed to the floor, still as a stone.

ALESSA

"Are you sure you want to do it yourself?"

"Are you kidding?" I laughed as I pulled the harness up my legs. Fastening it around my waist, I put the locking carabiners in place and ran my hands across the rope to ensure it was properly tied onto the rappelling structure.

"Of course I want to do it."

My foreman, Tameron, looked at me with a disapproving glance, both hands on his hips as he shook his head.

"Most engineers I know are glad to remain behind their desk, you know?" Grabbing my hand, he helped me over the bridge steel railings.

He didn't look too happy about the fact that I was

doing something he saw as being part of his job, but he knew better than to complain.

"I'm not like most engineers you know," I threw right back at him. I lowered my center of gravity until my body was parallel with the Sauma river, a mass of turbulent waters 800 feet below, and pressed my feet against the pillar in front of me.

Winking at Tameron, I eased the hold I had on the rope and allowed my body to go down, my knees locked as I made my descent.

Not really a fan of heights, I kept my gaze on the pillar and my feet. I could hear the water rippling from underneath me, a steady breeze whipping at the hair that escaped from my helmet, but I just ignored it all and kept on going down.

Tameron was right—most engineers would leave a task such as this to their underlings—but I never really cared to be a pencil pusher.

I liked being in the middle of the action, even if that meant facing my fear of heights.

Besides, being that I was younger than most engineers in charge of such big projects, I had to prove my mettle to the crew.

"Alright," I muttered once I had dropped almost 200 feet, gripping the rope tightly so that I'd stop in place. Narrowing my eyes, I looked at the bolts in the temporary steel frame supporting the pillar.

Someone had messed up, it seemed—the steel bolts they had put in place weren't the ones I had ordered to be used, and that meant we would have to replace this entire structure. That, of course, would translate as an inevitable delay.

"Pull me up," I cried out, looking up the pillar. From where I was, I couldn't see any of my workers, but I knew they could hear me. Except it seemed that they couldn't. I remained hanging there for a couple of seconds before reaching for the radio in my belt. Careful not to let go of the rope, I turned the radio on.

"What the hell are you doin' up there, Tameron? Pull me up. I've figured out the problem already."

I got nothing but the crackle of radio static.

The damn assholes were already probably lost in conversation, trying to arrange another nightly gathering of poker. As much as I liked this crew, I had to keep on top of them at all times, or else nothing would ever get done.

Not that I had any reason to complain—aside from this minor screw-up, everything was going perfectly.

I took a deep breath, calming my mind. All throughout my childhood, my flareups had been extraordinary. Finally my parents had enrolled me in martial arts.

It'd hadn't been the perfect solution, but the tools it had given me kept me steady.

Steadier.

And hitting something really hard did wonders for my temper.

This was workable.

Sure, we'd have to ask for a one week extension on our deadline, but that wasn't anything to worry about. Months of delays were perfectly natural in jobs of this nature, especially with all the logistic mess this damn continent turned into after the war.

"Tameron?" I insisted. "Do you copy?"

Exhaling sharply, I realized I would have to hoist myself up. Not an easy task, but I would gladly do it just so I could skin Tameron alive. I couldn't believe he got distracted and left me hanging while knowing that—

"Shit," I cried out, the rope losing some of its tension and sending me down a dozen feet. My feet lost their grip on the pillar, and I balanced from the rope like a sack of potatoes someone had slung over the bridge.

"What the hell are you assholes doin' up there?" I cried out while trying to grab the radio. My fingers were clammy and, as I tightened them around the plastic, it slipped from my fingers and the radio dropped into the river below.

I felt a knot form in my throat as I followed the radio with my gaze, nothing but a black dot being swallowed up by the rabid foam of a merciless river. I always tried not to look down when rappelling, but this time it was unavoidable—I was staring straight down at the abyss.

My heart thrashed inside my chest, and adrenaline started coursing through my veins like battery acid. It was hard to breathe, let alone think straight. "You got this, Alessa, you got this," I repeated over and over again, a stupid little mantra I hoped would calm me down. Foot by foot, I started making the climb up. My body was covered in sweat, my drenched clothes sticking to my body, but I kept going all the same.

"Hang on, Alessa," I finally heard a familiar voice cry out, and I looked up to see Tameron peeking over the railings. From the distance I couldn't really make out his face, but judging by his tone of voice I could tell he was panicking. What the hell was going on up there?

My body relaxed as I started feeling the pull of the rope once more, and I suddenly went up the pillar faster and faster. I didn't even care that the rope was biting into my ungloved hands. All I cared about was making it over the edge, safe and sound.

"I got you," Tameron muttered once I was within reach. Taking my hand, he hoisted me over the railings and I immediately collapsed on the floor, exhaustion finally taking over me. I sat on the ground, elbows resting on my knees, and I took deep breaths as I waited for the adrenaline to run its course.

"What the hell just happened?" I finally asked, somehow managing to push myself up to my feet.

Raking one hand over my face, I looked straight at Tameron, and my stomach lurched the moment I saw the deep creases on his forehead. He was my foreman because he *never* panicked, nor did he stress over things.

He was the kind of man you could count on when things got tough, and he always kept his head over his shoulders. Now, though, there was fear etched deep on his face.

"I don't know, Alessa, I really don't," he whispered, looking down at his feet as he spoke. Running one hand through his thinning hair, he finally looked into my eyes and pursed his lips. "They just up and left, the lot of 'em."

"What do you mean they up and left?"

"See for yourself," he continued, waving with his hand at one end of the bridge. I spun around and, shading my eyes from the sun with one hand, watched as dozens of workers dragged their feet toward some point in the distance. They were ambling in an uncoordinated way, the soles of their heavy boots dragging across the concrete, and they didn't seem to be paying attention to anything on their way.

There were other workers there, handling the machinery on the clearing by the end of the bridge, and they just shuffled out of the way as the group of runaway workers made their way past them.

"It happened all of a sudden," Tameron said, his voice low. "A few were handling the ropes, others were just milling around, and then…" He hesitated for a moment, shifted his weight from one foot to the other, and breathed out. "I don't know what came over them. They just dropped their tools, all at the same time, and started walking out."

"All of them?"

"Almost all of them," he replied. "Some, like me, kept our wits about us. But the rest of them just lost it. I tried talking to them, shouting their names, and I even stood in their way and tried to stop them. They wouldn't budge. They just kept on walking and walking, almost as if there's something in the jungle calling for them."

I opened my mouth to say something but, in the end, just remained silent. Whatever was going on wasn't normal, that was for sure.

"What should we do?" Tameron asked me.

"Let 'em go," I said, watching as the group of dazed workers kept on walking through the clearing and disappeared out into the jungle, their discoordinated bodies swallowed up by the thick green foliage. Wherever they were going, it wouldn't be safe for any of the other workers to follow. "We have no idea what's going on, and I'm not going to risk the rest of our crew." Taking a deep breath, I straightened my back and started walking down the bridge.

"Where are you going?" Tameron asked, and I didn't even bother looking back at him to reply.

"What do you think?" I threw back at him, doing my best not to let anxiety spread its wings inside me. "I'm going to call this in."

NAVAT

The woman only raised more questions and created more cause for concern the longer we observed her. After the Thermal test, she essentially went comatose.

Weird thing was, her eyes were open.

"We have to go in," Dr. Parr insisted. "She needs help."

"Can we verify that the Gorgo is gone?" Sakev asked.

"I think I saw it leave," I said.

"But can you be sure?"

"Are any of us sure of anything in this situation?" I fired back.

"That's my point," Sakev exclaimed. "If a Gorgo

decides to use one of us as a host, our entire operation is fucked."

"We can't just leave her there," Amira insisted. "She's our only shot at understanding what just happened."

"Grab the gas masks," Dr. Parr said decisively.

"Will that help?" Amira lifted a brow.

"I don't know but it'll make me feel better. Leena?"

Leena nodded and retrieved two gas masks from the emergency supply cupboard on the far end of the room.

"Grab a third one," I called to her. "I'm going in with you."

"Let me go," Sakev insisted. "Evie's my mate. I should be in there protecting her."

"That's why you shouldn't," I argued. "I can be more objective in this situation than you can."

"He's got a point," Amira pursed her lips.

"If I'm in there, I need someone monitoring readings from out here." Dr. Parr tapped the top of her datapad. "I'll need both hands when I'm in here. Sakev, I've taught you how to read this kind of stuff."

Dr. Parr flipped the datapad around to reveal charts filled with jagged lines, rows of numbers, and a slew of other stuff I didn't understand.

"I need you to tell me what's happening on her insides while I'm in there," she said.

"Can do," Sakev nodded.

Leena tossed me a gas mask.

"I hope this does something," I muttered and I slipped it on.

"We don't know how Gorgos infect their hosts. Could be an airborne virus type of deal," Leena said.

"That's enough for me. Let's do this."

I opened the door to the reinforced cell. If the woman on the floor was aware of the movement, she didn't react. Her blank gaze was fixed on the ceiling above. She stared right into one of the fluorescent lights, unblinking.

"Ma'am?" Dr. Parr called out. "I'm a doctor. I'm here to help you. Can you tell me if you feel any pain?"

To no one's surprise, the woman didn't answer.

"She looks dehydrated," Evie said, tilting her head to one side. The three of us looked creepy as skrell standing here with the gas masks over our faces. We're probably the last thing that woman wanted to see.

"Maybe the Gorgo's don't know what a human host body needs," Leena said. "That could be why they abandon their hosts so quickly."

"I don't think so," I frowned.

Leena turned her steely gaze on me.

"Elaborate."

"The Gorgo's are strong enough to suck the life out of things like the Puppet Master, right?" I said. "The Puppet Master is strong, too strong to be taken down by brute force alone. The Gorgo's have to be strategic in the way they suck the life out of the other Puppet Masters which implies they're capable of studying and learning about their hosts."

"But did the Gorgo's actively inhabit the Puppet Master's family?" Leena asked.

"I don't know," I admitted.

"None of us know anything," Dr. Parr sighed.

She knelt down beside the woman and checked her pulse.

"She's alive but her pulse is weak," she said. "She really needs fluids. Can we have some brought in?"

"I'll make the call," Sakev said from the outside.

"Can you call Sk'lar in here as well?" I asked. "I think he'll want to see this."

Sakev nodded and spoke rapidly into his radio.

"Help me," a rasping voice said. I turned my attention back to the woman.

"Help me," the voice came again. It had to be from the woman, it couldn't have been from anyone else. Yet, her lips weren't moving. Her eyes showed no sign of awareness.

"Is that her?"

"I think so," Dr. Parr said, looking just as perplexed as I felt.

"She looks...drier," Leena said.

"Hosting the Gorgo took too much out of her," Dr. Parr's voice sounded thick. "It's desperately trying to make up for the depleted resources but it's not working."

"And her mouth isn't moving when she speaks because?" I prompted.

"I can't help you there," Dr. Parr clicked her tongue. "Maybe we can ask her when she comes around."

"I don't think that's going to happen," Leena said softly.

I looked back at the woman. Somehow, she looked even more vacant than she had a second ago. I knew she was gone.

"What a shame," I murmured.

"Let's get her into the medical wing for an autopsy," Leena sighed heavily. Dr. Parr said nothing.

"You wanted to see me, Navat?" Sk'lar's voice took my attention off the dead woman. The rest of Strike Team Three followed him into the room. A nice surprise.

I exited the holding cell while Sakev helped Leena bring in a stretcher. Dr. Parr knelt beside the woman. Her lips moved but I couldn't hear her speech. I wondered what she was saying.

"I wanted you to witness this subject first hand," I said. "But there's no point. She just died."

"Oh," Sk'lar's face fell. "What killed her?"

"I think it was the force of the Gorgo leaving her body," I said. "Though, we still haven't verified that she was a host. We didn't get a chance to verify anything, actually."

"Did you observe anything unusual?"

"She was calm while she was brought in," I reported. "She didn't fight the scouts. She only acted up when we started the thermal test and even then, her aggression didn't seem to be directed at us."

Sk'lar furrowed his brow.

"That's the most non-invasive test. Why would she react so negatively to it?"

"I have a theory," Amira piped up.

"By all means." Sk'lar made a sweeping gesture with his hand.

"Assuming she was infested with a Gorgo," Amira started, "I think it knew what we were doing."

"You mean, it knew we were testing for its presence?" Sk'lar asked.

"Exactly. It didn't freak out until we started actively searching for it," she continued. "I think it started forcing the host to hurt herself in an attempt to make us stop testing."

Sk'lar looked to me.

"Makes sense to me," I shrugged.

"That goes against known Gorgo behavior," Cazak said thoughtfully.

"What little we have, that is," Jalok added.

"I've never seen a Gorgo fight to avoid detection, let

alone fight to keep a specific host," Sk'lar said. "They usually discard a host soon after inhabiting it. They don't take care to avoid detection."

"Maybe there was something specific about this woman." I gestured to the body leaving the room on a stretcher. I didn't even know her name. I shook off a wave of disgust for the Gorgos. "Maybe they aren't just taking over the bodies, they're also harvesting knowledge."

"We don't have anything that supports that theory," Amira said.

"Except we do," I countered. "All of those scientists out in the Sika Jungle that came up against Tyehn and Maki were taken over by Gorgos and were used for something specific. It's a fair bet the Gorgo sought those scientists out."

Amira narrowed her eyes.

"What did you say your background was?"

"Construction," I answered. "Why?"

"You're wasted in that field," she said. "Should've been a detective."

"A what?"

"A human puzzle solver," she clarified. "One that catches criminals."

"Sounds boring."

Amira snorted.

"Do you think we could compile a list of humans

with useful traits?" Jalok asked. "We could be proactive and put those people into protective custody."

"Everyone on this planet has some kind of useful trait," Amira said. "We're a young colony world. We aren't established enough for people to sit around in their summer homes and do nothing. Everyone here still pulls their weight in some way or another."

"That might be why they narrowed in on this planet," I said. "If there are other Puppet Masters out there, why is ours such a big draw? The accomplished human population is likely a factor."

"But to what end? Sk'lar asked. "How much can the Gorgo's expect to accomplish if they keep draining and discarding their hosts?"

"Maybe they're taking the knowledge even when the body shuts down," Tyhen suggested.

"That's possible," Sk'lar nodded. "Prevention should be our first priority, nonetheless."

"What about extraction?" I asked. "We can prevent all we want but we still can't narrow down how the Gorgo's get into their hosts. We ran a thermal test on that woman and the Gorgo fled. Surely, that means something?"

"Yes, but it killed her when it fled," Sk'lar replied. "We can't let that happen to everyone who ends up a host."

"We need another subject to run tests on." Amira

gnawed on the inside of her cheek. "Until then, we're just running on theories and making guesses."

"What else is new?" I laughed. "We've been running on theories and educated guesses since the *Vengeance* smashed into this rock. We should be old pros at this by now."

"Glad you can still find something to laugh about, Navat," Sk'lar gave me a stern look but it didn't knock the smile off my face. If I didn't find the humor in situations like this, I'd be a seething pile of anger at all hours. No one wanted that, least of all me.

I'd gotten good at finding the humor in even the bleakest of situations. I'd had an entire lifetime to perfect the art of it. I wasn't about to stop now.

ALESSA

"I don't think I've ever seen you like this."

"What? Do I look bad?" Cocking one eyebrow up, I looked down at the gray pencil skirt I was wearing. It wasn't just the skirt, though—I was also wearing a white blouse and a nice pair of high heels. Not my attire of preference, but I had to play it safe. "Just trying to look professional. They're not gonna be too happy about this."

"It's not like we're to blame," Tameron shrugged.

"And do you think they're gonna care?"

"Yeah, you're right," he breathed out, leaning against his seat and folding his arms over his chest. Resting his head against the wall, he closed his eyes and quickly fell asleep. It didn't matter where we were, Tameron always managed to magically fall asleep whenever he wanted to. I had no idea how he did it, but it was a useful skill to have whenever you had to wait for hours on end—and that was exactly what we were doing.

After the incident at the Sauma river, I was immediately called for an emergency meeting with my boss and all the guys backing the project financially. The bridge I was building was supposed to connect two neighboring towns that relied on land traffic, and commerce had taken a heavy hit after all other bridges were destroyed during the war. Businessmen, most of them merchants from those two towns, had poneyed up the money to have another bridge built, and they hadn't been too happy to find out almost half of my crew had walked out without warning.

Now Tameron and I were waiting in a decrepit lobby while my boss was holed up in a conference room, doing his best to keep the investors from going nuts. If they pulled the plug now, the construction company I worked for would be in deep trouble.

"They'll see you now, Ms. Naro," a young receptionist appeared in the lobby, clutching a folder against her chest. She was young, probably around my age, and had that air of impersonal professionalism that most receptionists had. I stood up, punched Tameron in the arm, and watched him rise to his feet. "I'm afraid they've just asked for you, Ms. Naro," the receptionist continued, awkwardly biting on the corner of her lips.

"Alright," I nodded, not sure on what to make of it. As my foreman, Tameron accompanied me to most of the meetings I had to take.

The fact that the investors only wanted to see me didn't bode well. "Wait here, this shouldn't take long."

"We'll see about that," he grumbled, sinking into his seat once more. I still hadn't turned around and he had already closed his eyes and gone back to sleep. Taking a deep breath, I nodded at the receptionist once more and followed after her as she led the way into the conference room.

"Good luck, Ms. Naro," she whispered as she held the doors open for me, offering me a little smile as I passed through. Returning her smile, I stepped into the room to see almost twenty men sitting around a large glass table. Most of them were old and fat, but there were some that still seemed to be a few years away from middle-age. My boss, Alberon Zorne, sat between two of the oldest guys, and he didn't look comfortable in the slightest.

A fifty-year-old man that had built a successful company from the ground up, he now had to fight tooth-and-nail for every single contract we landed. You'd think that war and destruction would be a boon for a construction company, but when people suddenly don't have enough money to pay for the pre-war contracts, financial survival becomes a real struggle.

"Please, take a seat, Alessa," he said, pointing at the empty seat right across from where he was. Slowly, I did as I was told and sat down, carefully folding my hands in front of me as I waited for someone to address me.

"Mr. Zorne has informed us of what happened in the Sauma river," one of the guys sitting beside Alberon said. He had a long beard with streaks of white and, even though he wasn't sitting at the head of the table, he seemed like he was chairing the meeting. "We passed all the information you provided to the government, and we have been informed that similar situations have been happening in various cities."

"Similar situations?" I echoed, not sure on what I was being told. I had spent the last few weeks living on a small tent by the edge of the jungle, while working on the bridge, and I wasn't exactly keeping up to date with the news. "What exactly has been happening?"

"It's too early to say, I think," the man continued, running his pudgy fingers through his long beard. "Apparently it's all because of the Gorgos."

"And what the hell is a Gorgo?" I asked, the words escaping from between my lips before I had the time to filter them. Had I become stupid overnight or something? I wasn't understanding a damn thing.

"No one's really sure," someone to my side said. This one was younger than the chairman, although he still had at least ten years on me. He was wearing a tailored suit, and there was a massive ring on his right hand, one that he tapped against the table as he spoke.

"The government is keeping a lid on things, presumably to stop everyone from panicking. From what I've gathered, the Gorgos are an alien species that act as a parasite. Just like a virus. They attach themselves to their human hosts, and take over them."

Sighing heavily, I leaned back in my chair and closed my eyes.

More aliens? Just great.

"So you're saying that half my crew was possessed by some parasitic alien?" I asked, shaking my head as I said it.

The entire planet had been turned upside down after the *Vengeance* guys got here, no doubt about it. Ever since their arrival, there was always something funky and dangerous happening every week.

War against the Xathi, vine domes, protests and rebellion...it seemed like the madness would never end.

"What are we going to do about it?"

"I got word from the capital that they're investigating," the chairman replied. "Not much else we can do about it. In the meantime, we still have that bridge to build."

"Alright, alright," I whispered, trying to process all

that information without going nuts. "I'm gonna need to hire some more workers to compensate for the—"

"That's been taken care of, Alessa," my boss cut me short. "You've been assigned a completely new team."

"What's that supposed to mean?" I frowned. "Some of them walked out, sure, but a lot of them are still there, waiting for construction to continue. They're not to blame, you know? Even though their friends and colleagues walked out into the jungle, these guys remained on their posts."

"It's not about blame, Alessa. Thing is, Gorgos only seem to affect humans."

"So?"

"So that's why your new team will be made up of Skotans."

"You've gotta be kidding me," I said, looking around the table to see if someone shared my disbelief. Apparently, not. They had come to this decision before I had even stepped one foot inside the room, and there wasn't anything I could say to make them go back on it. "How am I supposed to train a new team from scratch? Especially if they're aliens? They probably have no experience in construction. You can't expect me to—"

"Alessa, I get it," Alberon interrupted me again, except this time he did it in a soothing manner. "I helped vet your new team. They all have experience when it comes to construction, and they're fast learners. You don't have to worry about anything like that, alright?"

Running one hand through my hair, I just exhaled sharply.

"Can we count on you to finish the bridge, Ms. Naro?" The bearded chairman spoke up, looking me straight in the eyes. I was of half-a-mind to tell him to go build it himself, but saner minds prevailed.

"Yeah, alright," I said as I pushed my chair back and stood up. "I'll go build your damn bridge." With that, I turned around and left, my heels clicking against the polished floor like the hand of a clock. The moment Tameron saw me stepping into the lobby, he jumped to his feet as if there were springs under his boots.

"So, how did that go?"

"Not great," I merely said, not knowing how I'd break the news.

The poor guy had a family to feed, and now I would have to tell him he'd have to pack his bags and go back home without a steady paycheck.

"Spit it out, Alessa."

"They're getting me a new team."

"Well, that's good, isn't it?"

"You didn't hear me," I said. "It's a brand new team. Skotans from the *Vengeance*, the lot of them."

"Oh, fuck."

"Yeah," I smiled sadly. "That's the word."

NAVAT

The day after the incident with the infected woman whose name I still didn't know, I walked through Command Central on my way to get my assignments for the day, mind whirling.

I'd spent all night, wide-awake, puzzling over the Gorgos. I didn't like going to sleep with unsolved problems.

Unfortunately for me, the Gorgo problem wasn't one that could be solved in one night.

"Navat!" I heard Tyehn's voice behind me.

"Need something?" I asked when he caught up to me.

"I'm heading out to the Sika Jungle with Maki today," he said. "There are still some humans out there. Do you want to come along?"

"Why me?" I asked.

"You had some solid theories about the Gorgos yesterday. I figured if you spent time around the crater they were digging, you and I could get somewhere."

"I have to see what my assignments are for the day." I started walking once more.

"I already suggested to Sk'lar that you head out with us," Tyehn said.

"Did you?" I folded my arms over my chest.

"Yes. Why do you look like you're about to punch my teeth in?"

"To freak you out. Come on. Let's go."

"You have an odd sense of humor."

"I know. It keeps me on my toes." I clapped him on the back and turned toward the elevators.

Maki was waiting for us at the hanger.

"I've already packed up everything we're going to need," she declared.

"Weapons?" I asked.

"Stun guns," she replied.

"Are you sure that's all we'll need?"

Maki placed a hand on her hip.

"At the end of the day, our biggest threat is encased in a human body. Do you really want to blow it's brains out, especially when you know Evie and Leen need more test subjects?"

"When you put it that way, no."

"That's what I thought. Don't worry. These stun guns are strong enough to take down a rampaging Phetnes."

"I'm assuming that's a name for a strong nightmarish creature you've got roaming this planet."

"You'd assume correctly. They don't like jungles so we won't have to worry about them but my point still stands."

Mika swung herself up into the aerial unit. It was a compact little thing with a swooping propeller on top. It looked old but nowhere near broken down.

"Looks like we're all set," Tyehn nodded with approval and climbed up into the pilot's seat.

"You're flying us?" I snorted.

"Yes, I am. Scared?"

"Concerned. I'd prefer not to crash today. Once in this lifetime was enough for me."

I climbed into one of the passenger seats. It wasn't an exaggeration to say I was spilling out of it.

"Was this seat made for a child?"

"No, it was made for a normal-sized human," Maki quipped.

"Don't close the door," I warned Tyehn. "You'll slice my leg off."

"Good thing there isn't a door."

Tyehn powered on the aerial unit. We lifted straight

off the ground. Wind whipped around me as my leg dangled out of the open side.

"How did this win out as our primary mode of transportation?" I asked as we shot away from the city in the direction of the jungle. "Don't we have rifts for a reason?"

"This is more fun," Tyehn called over the roaring wind.

"Oh! Well as long as you're enjoying yourself," I grumbled back.

Maki laughed as the wind whipped her hair around her face.

"What's the plan once we get there?" I shouted.

"What?" Maki shouted back.

"The plan!"

"What?"

"Never mind."

"What?"

I glared at Maki only to receive a shit-eating grin in response.

Somehow, I was the one with the twisted sense of humor.

Tyehn brought the aerial unit down in a clearing and powered down the engine.

"What's the plan?" I asked again.

"We're going to go to the camp," he explained.

"And then?"

"We'll see what we find."

"That's not a plan. That's an idea."

"My plan is to follow the idea," he replied.

"What if there are hostile humans?" I prompted.

"That's what the stun guns are for."

"I think we should set up a perimeter and observe from afar before we stroll right on up to them," I suggested.

Maki tilted her head in my direction.

"He's got a point."

"Oh, and you've always been the cautious one?" Tyehn gave her a sly grin.

"Cautious? No. But I don't like to be outright stupid."

"All right," Tyehn tossed his hands in the air. "The three of us will set up the planet's smallest three-person perimeter and go from there."

We walked together through the forest until we neared the camp. Maki and Tyehn walked to the west. I made my way to the east.

"See anything?" I called into the radio after walking about half a mile.

"The new batch of scientists," Maki replied. "Nothing looks out of the ordinary."

"How many?"

"A dozen or so," she said.

"Any telltale signs of Gorgos?"

"They look healthy from here," Tyehn reported. "But its not exactly like they come with bright labels."

"Okay. Let's move in."

I moved closer to the scientist's camp until they came into view. Maki and Tyehn's observations appeared to be accurate. None of the known signs of Gorgo interference were present.

"Greetings!" I called out.

A few of the scientists jumped at the sound of my voice but no one reacted with aggression.

"My apologies for startling you," I grinned. "We're from General Rouhr's company."

"What do you want?"

"To help, of course," Maki stepped out of the clearing.

"Help? You're sneaking around with weapons. That doesn't sound helpful." A young male scientist who made Leena look downright cuddly narrowed his eyes at us.

"For all we knew, you'd fallen to the Gorgos."

He furrowed his brow.

"The what?"

"It's something we're trying to prevent and learn more about in the process," Maki explained.

"That's not good enough," the young man. "If you want access to our site, which is highly confidential by the way, you need to spill it."

"Spill what?" Tyehn blinked in confusion.

"Did you hear about what happened to the first teams that came out here?" Maki asked.

"We know they were infected by something," the man sniffed. "We've gone to measures to prevent that."

"You can't block out the things that infected them," Maki explained. "We don't even fully understand what they are yet."

"We call them Gorgos," I explained.

"That sounds made up."

"All names are made up," I replied. "My point is, we aren't here to steal your work or get in your way. We're here to make sure you're all safe and to figure out what's so special about this place."

"We're safe," he sighed.

"Great!" I clapped my hands together. "Now we can focus on the second part."

"Tyehn, Navat, come look at this."

While I was talking to the scientist, Maki had wandered closer to the hole dug by those affected by the Gorgos. I stepped up to the edge of the ditch beside her.

"What am I looking at?" I asked.

"I'm not sure." She tapped her finger against her chin. "But answer me this. Why do you dig a hole in the first place?"

"To bury something," I said.

"Or dig up something that's already buried," Tyehn finished.

"Exactly," Maki nodded. "I bet there's something down here."

"Excuse me!" The scientist scurried over. "You're not authorized to do anything here."

"That's where you're wrong," Tyehn grinned. He passed a keycard to the scientist. "Check this for yourself. You'll see we all have the highest level of security clearance. We can sleep in that hole if we wanted to."

"Which we don't." Maki wrinkled her nose.

The scientist took the key card and scanned it with his wrist device. It flashed green.

"Well," he said primly. "I suppose I can't legally stop you but I'll be watching like a hawk."

"Good," Maki grinned. "You'll want to see this."

"See what?" said Tyehn, the scientist and myself in unison.

"Navat, do me a favor and radio the Urai," Maki said. "I want to order a satellite scan of the area."

"We've already done that," the scientist said. "The scans turned up nothing useful."

"But do you have Urai tech?" Maki smirked.

"No," the scientist muttered.

"That's what I thought. Don't worry. The scan won't damage anything beneath the surface."

"It better not."

Once I felt certain the scientist had finished protesting, I grabbed my radio.

"What do you want?" Came Fen's voice.

"Fen, always a pleasure," I grinned. "You sound like you're in a good mood."

"This may be a shock to you, but I don't sit around at my desk all day waiting for you and yours to need something."

"Yet you answered."

"What do you want?"

"Can you send a satellite over to my coordinates? We're looking for something beneath the earth."

"How deep?"

I looked to Tyehn and Maki, who shrugged. The scientist didn't look like he knew either.

"I don't have all day."

"You really are a delight, you know that?" I smirked. "Let's call it three hundred meters."

"Whatever you like."

"Thank you, Fen. You're the best."

"I know."

She clicked off the channel and I sent her my coordinates. She sent back a live tracker for the satellite she sent.

"You seem like a real charmer," the scientist said to me.

"I get the job done," I shrugged.

"I've never heard Fen be so prickly," Tyehn said. "What did you do to piss her off?"

"I may have referred to her as my personal transportation service," I said.

"Brave. Stupid, but brave. You're lucky she hasn't tried to chop off your arm via rift."

"She's tried. Three times."

"Ah," Tyehn nodded. "Well, when I find your body sliced in half one of these days, I'll know why."

"Please bury the halves together when you find them."

"What makes you think I'll go looking?"

We laughed while the scientist looked between us with a mixture of annoyance and confusion on his narrow face.

"Don't mind them," Maki said. "That's a normal conversation."

"Just find me when the scans come in," the scientist replied before stomping off.

I watched him walk away.

"He seems like a real charmer."

Maki snorted. "As long as he's not possessed, we can work with it, right?"

ALESSA

Beads of sweat trickled down my brow, the morning sun mercilessly whipping the earth with its heat. Running one hand through my hair, I shaded my eyes from the sun and leaned against one of the bridge's steel beams.

From underneath me I could hear the roaring waters of the Sauma river, and I couldn't resist the urge to lean over the edge and gaze at them.

Building a bridge over such turbulent waters hadn't been an easy task, but it was finally done. Even though the investors had been hesitant to fund such an undertaking, my plans and schematics were now a part of the real world. Four lanes wide, it was a long puzzle of steel and cables, its arches perfect semi-circles that had started as mathematical equations.

It would stand the test of time, I was sure of it. No matter what happened, people would still be walking across it a hundred years from now. I doubted anyone would remember my name by then, but I didn't care much about it. My legacy was made of steel and concrete, and I was ready for it to outlast my own reputation.

"We've just finished testing the structure," I heard someone say beside me, and I spun around to find a tall Skotan standing there. He wasn't wearing a helmet, as the regulations mandated, nor was he wearing a yellow vest. Instead, he had a simple grey shirt, one that was covered with dust and small pieces of rock. On his waist was a large belt crammed with all sorts of tools.

"And?"

"It all checks out," he said. "I've left the reports on your desk in case you want to double-check." The aliens weren't exactly the best when it came to following the safety protocols on a building site, but I had to hand it to them—they were a competent bunch.

Whenever I told them to do something, they did it flawlessly and without complaint. More than just that, they didn't mind the fact that I was a woman.

The only thing they cared about was my knowledge. That was refreshing.

"Thank you," I said with a nod. "You can radio Alberon and tell him we're done." Usually it would fall on me to radio the boss such big news, but this time I was ready to break tradition.

Alberon had insisted on the alien crew, so I figured he wouldn't mind if it was one of them making the announcement.

It was a petty thing for me to do, but I didn't like the fact that a crew had been imposed on me. Even if those guys were competent, I liked picking my own team.

"Already did it," the Skotan said in that deep tone of his, his right hand hooked on his tool belt. "He's on his way here to see it for himself."

"You shouldn't have told him without my say-so," I frowned. As foreman of the building site, it was within his purview to do what he did, but I didn't like it.

Whenever I had to handle a project as large as this, I liked to remain in control of every single thing that happened on site. Micromanaging isn't exactly one of my best qualities, but there are times when I just can't help it.

"The job is done," he shrugged, and then just turned on his heels and started walking down the bridge. He unbuckled his belt as he went, and slung it over his shoulder in a casual manner. I followed him with my gaze until he joined the rest of the crew, more than fifty men -aliens, whatever - resting under the shade of the forest, right on the other side of the bridge, and let out a heavy sigh.

I still wasn't sure what to make of them. They were good workers, but they had a way of going about things that I wasn't used to.

Efficiency was something I valued, no two ways about it, but I still wasn't used to not having humans around.

"Let it go, Alessa," I muttered under my breath. The crew had done an impressive job, and the bridge was already done.

There was no use in dwelling on things now. With some luck, there'd be some time between my next project, and Alberon would see the light and give me the all-human crew I wanted.

Wiping the sweat off my brow, I started making my way across the bridge. I always liked doing a little speech whenever a project was completed, especially when my crew deserved some praise, and I wasn't about to change that just because these guys were aliens.

Good workers deserve respect, even if they weren't my first choice.

Once I closed in on the group, I climbed onto a transport truck and stood on its hood, hands on my hips as I allowed my gaze to take them all in.

"We made it," I started to say, and almost every single one of them stood up straight to hear me. It was slightly disconcerting. Human crews were hit-or-miss when it came to respecting a female supervisor, so having them all stand at attention just because I said a couple of words was something I wasn't used to. "And we did it on schedule. I can tell you that Alberon and the investors were expecting delays and extra-costs, but we've managed to pull this off without a hitch. And all thanks to you."

I was about to continue when the roar of a loud engine took over our surroundings, and a sudden breeze whipped my hair back.

Reacting on instinct, I looked up to see a small transport shuttle cutting its way across the blue sky, its engines on a feeble truce with gravity as it made its way down.

"Looks like the boss is here," I cried out, hoping the guys would hear me, and jumped out of the truck. I waited as the shuttle landed on a nearby clearing and, once the engines were killed, I started making my way toward it.

Alberon climbed out from it a moment later, the sleeves of his white shirt rolled to his elbows. He was wearing dress pants and impeccably polished shoes, but no tie. Even though he was a corporate animal, he enjoyed dressing down a little whenever he came to meet his troops.

"Alessa, I'm impressed," he said as we met, immediately reaching for my hand and shaking it. "I wasn't expecting to hear from you for another week or two. The investors were ready to pony up some extra money to see this happen, you know?"

"I can give them my bank account number, if they're that eager to part with their money," I said with a smile. Even though Alberon was my boss, our relationship was a friendly one. He knew I was essential to the success of his building company, and I depended on him for a steady stream of interesting projects I could work on. Our success needed that friendly trust.

"You're in a good mood, huh?" He laughed. "Come, walk with me. I wanna see this bridge of yours."

"It's more yours than mine," I said, walking after him as he made his way toward the bridge. We walked side by side until we were standing in the middle of it and, just like I had done earlier before, Alberon leaned over the edge and glanced at the river down below.

"You've done an excellent job here, Alessa." Leaning against the railings, he folded his arms over his chest and smiled at me. "I know this project was harder than the rest, with all the craziness that's been happening, and I think I might persuade the investors to provide you with a nice bonus. You like the sound of that?"

"A bonus? Damn right I like the sound of that," I laughed. "But, really, I just want to move on to the next project. I don't like standing still."

"I'm sure we'll find something for you. With all the

rebuilding that's taking place across the continent, there are a lot of projects that wouldn't mind an experienced engineer at hand. It's just a matter of securing the right contracts."

"There's just one thing I'd like to ask you," I continued, shifting my weight from one foot to the other as I thought of what my next words would be. I didn't need to worry, because Alberon quickly realized what I was getting at.

"Oh, come on, Alessa, not this again," he sighed, shaking his head and placing both hands on his hips.

"I just want to choose my own crew."

"No, you just don't want to work with the aliens," he corrected me. "I seriously have no idea why's that an issue. They're extremely competent, they got this bridge done on schedule, and they respect you. Why don't you like working with them?

"I just don't," I insisted.

Truth be told, I had no better answer. I had been lucky, as my family had been left alone by the Xathi during the invasion, but I still couldn't wrap my head around how much things had changed after the aliens arrived here.

I accepted their presence as a fact of life, but that didn't mean I liked it.

My heart tightened every time I thought of all the

buildings I had helped build, most of them now turned into rubble, and all because of them.

"That's not a valid answer," Alberon said. Shaking his head once more, he sighed heavily. "I'll see what I can do, but no promises."

Well, that was something.

NAVAT

"I thought the Urai's tech was supposed to be advanced," the scientist, who had not warmed up to me at all in the past hour, huffed impatiently.

That was alright. I hadn't really warmed up to his scrawny self either.

"It is," Maki replied.

"Then why don't we have our results yet?"

"Our results?" I lifted a brow. "Now you want to be part of the team?"

"I'm the one with the team. Not you," he shot back.

"We're the ones with the satellite," I corrected.

"Don't worry, you'll be allowed to see the results of our work," Maki teased.

The scientist's face turned a concerning shade of

red. That was a man who needed a drink if I'd ever seen one.

Actually, a drink didn't sound too bad now that I thought about it.

A ping drew my attention to Maki.

"Results are in," she grinned.

The scientist scurried over to Maki with a greedy look in his eyes.

"What is it? What is it?" He demanded frantically.

I gave him a suspicious glance.

"Sir, I'm going to need you to take a step back."

"Excuse me?" he hissed. "This is my work."

"Look into my eyes," I ordered.

"Navat?" Tyehn gave me a curious look. "You don't think…" he trailed off.

"We can't be too careful," I shrugged.

"What are you talking about?" the scientists demanded.

"Just do as he says," Maki urged gently.

"Fine." The scientist fixed me with a withering glare that would've been quite intimidating if I were someone else.

And a child.

Who was easily frightened.

"His eyes look clear to me," I said.

"I agree," Maki said.

"What are you talking about?" the scientist demanded.

"He's not showing signs of aggression, just irritability," Tyehn said.

"No shit I'm irritable," the scientist spat. "You three just waltz in here and take over my camp and expect me to be calm about it?"

"The rest of your coworkers are calm," I observed.

"They don't have anything riding on this the way I do," he insisted.

"Like what?"

"I'm writing my thesis on this," he explained. "My standing in the scientific community depends on what I discover here. If I come up with piles of dirt, I'm nothing. I'm finished."

"That explains a lot," I muttered. "Okay, he's clear for signs of Gorgos, as far as I can tell."

"You thought I was one of them?" He shrieked.

"Can you blame us?" Maki gave him a look. "We're at the site of a massive Gorgo exposure. This is where some of the first people fell under their influence."

"I'm not one of them," he hissed. "I just want to see what's beneath the earth.'"

"Do you have somewhere where we can pull the image results up on a larger screen?" Maki asked.

"Follow me."

As if nothing happened, the scientist turned on his heel and stalked toward a cluster of tents.

"Talk about work-place stress," I sighed.

"And we thought fighting Xathi was intense," Tyehn joked.

We followed the scientist deeper into the camp. We passed his colleagues as we walked. Some nodded to us, others ignored us.

All of them gave the pushy little man a wide berth.

"How do we see the scans?" He asked once all four of us were in one of the tents. The far wall of the tent was completely covered in monitors displaying all kinds of charts and graphs.

"I'll connect to the Urai's network," Maki offered.

"I'd prefer if you didn't mess with my set up," the scientist said.

"Okay," I shrugged, my patience wearing thin. "We'll just head back to our labs and look at it there."

"Sounds good to me," Tyehn agreed.

"Wait!" The scientist cried out.

"What's the point, sir?" I asked. "You aren't going to give us access and we need to see what's on these scans. We're trying to work with you. I'd appreciate it if you tried to work with us as well."

"How diplomatic of you, Navat," Maki grinned.

"He's full of surprises, isn't he?"

I rolled my eyes at my companions.

The scientist stared at us for a long moment until I thought he was for sure going to kick us out of the workspace. Instead, he let out a sigh.

"Go ahead," he gestured to the set up. "But screw any of my data up and there will be hell to pay."

"I expect nothing less," I said.

Maki went to work accessing the Urai's network. From there, they connected her to the satellite.

As soon as the images appeared on the screen, we knew we'd stumbled onto something unusual.

"What is that?" Tyehn asked.

"I don't know," Maki shook her head. "Whatever it is, it's big."

The satellite image showed shadows beneath the earth perhaps fifty feet below the surface. The shadows were huge, indicating a large, dense structure. Judging from the images, it was two hundred meters long and perhaps one hundred and fifty meters wide.

The depth of the structure was hard to ascertain for certain, but it looked as if it penetrated rather deep into the earth. Another five hundred meters, maybe.

"How did the Gorgo know about this?" I wondered.

"Who knows?" Maki said. "I want to know why it's so important to them. We should call in a dig squad and start a proper excavation."

"Absolutely!" The scientist gushed. "I knew something was down there. I just knew it."

"Hold on a moment," Tyehn said. "I don't think we should go diving into that thing just yet."

"Why not?" Both Maki and the scientist demanded.

"What if there are toxic spores? What if there are traps? We have no idea what that thing is. We should do above-ground testing before we break out the shovels."

"I'm inclined to agree with Tyehn," I said. "If the Gorgos want it, I'm willing to bet it's something dangerous."

"If it's dangerous, shouldn't we get to it before the Gorgos have the chance?" Maki countered.

"What if the Gorgos have already gotten to it?" I replied. "What if there's already something down there, waiting for someone to carelessly disturb it? I'm not saying we should cover it up and walk away, I'm just saying we need to proceed with caution here."

"Exactly," Tyehn nodded.

"Remember what happened to Amira and Dax?" I asked. "They almost died in that underground temple because they had no idea what they were getting into. I don't want a repeat of that."

"What if that's what this is?" Maki's eyes lit up. "It could be another one of those temples."

"What temples? What are you talking about?" The scientist looked eagerly back and forth between us.

"Ever use rift travel?" Maki asked him.

"No, but I know what it is."

"Friends of ours found the device that makes rift traveling possible inside a temple out in the desert. We never figured out the temple's origins."

"Do you think another one of those devices could be down there?"

"Maybe," Maki shrugged. "It's impossible to tell from here." She turned back to face me and Tyehn. "Which is why we should get excavating before the Gorgo's send another horde after it."

"I'll inform General Rouhr," I said. "I'll see what he wants us to do."

"I'll arrange dig site preparations, just in case," Maki smirked.

"Fine," I sighed. "But don't confirm anything until General Rouhr gives the go-ahead. I don't want to pay out of pocket for diggers and sensors and whatever other nonsense you're thinking of bringing in here."

"You know me too well," Maki grinned. She turned to the scientist. "How do I get ahold of any of the major cities from here?"

"Follow me."

The two left the tent, leaving Tyhen and me behind.

"What are your thoughts?" He asked me.

"I think we're about to poke into something that was never meant to be disturbed," I replied.

"Cryptic," Tyehn barked out a laugh. "I'll go make sure Maki doesn't go overboard."

"Wise decision," I nodded.

I pulled out my radio and reached out to General Rouhr.

"That was quick," he said once I was patched through. "I wasn't expecting to hear anything so soon."

"We've found what appears to be a large structure buried beneath the earth," I reported. "Initial scans don't give us much to go on. Maki wants to start excavating as soon as possible."

"Was there anything concerning on the scans?" General Rouhr asked.

"Only that we can't confirm anything about the structure," I replied. "The scans were taken by one of the Urai satellites. You should be able to pull them up on your console."

"Excellent." General Rouhr went quiet as he pulled up the scans. "Oh. Yes, I see what you mean. That's remarkably large, whatever it is."

"We're theorizing that it's another temple," I said. "Like the one Amira and Dax discovered."

"Reasonable," General Rouhr said thoughtfully. "Well, I see no unusual energy signatures or heat markers. I authorize you to bring in a dig team and get to work."

"Maki is already making preparations. Hopefully, we'll make progress before sundown."

"Good. I'm going to send someone over who might

be able to give you some insight," he said. "Expect them in a few hours."

"I'll make arrangements," I said.

"I expect frequent reports as this matter develops."

"Yes, sir."

ALESSA

"He's already expecting you," the blonde receptionist smiled. Leaning on her chair, she pointed at the office door behind her, motioning me to walk in.

"Thank you," I said, returning her smile as I walked past her and into Alberon's office. He was sitting behind an old mahogany desk, one that was littered with all kinds of documents and schematics.

His office was old and cramped, but he always assured me that soon enough we'd start building a new office building and move there. The old one had been destroyed during the war, which forced him to move his company into a rundown building on the outskirts of town. Much like other companies, the war had put us through financial hell.

"Glad you could make it in such short notice, Alessa." Raising his head, he looked at me and drummed his fingers against the edge of his desk.

"It's not like I was busy," I said as I sat across him. "What's this about? You got a new job for me?" It had been almost a week since I had finished the bridge, and I was starting to get antsy. I needed to keep moving, or else I'd go mad. Alberon was always trying to convince me to go on holidays, but I always refused.

"That's right." Leafing through a stack of documents, he grabbed one of them and slid it across the desk. "It's not your usual thing, but I think you're going to like it all the same. It's an interesting job, to say the least."

"If you say so," I muttered, grabbing the document and glancing at it. The location given for the job was the Sika jungle, which was odd. "What's this about? Are we gonna start building things in the middle of absolutely nowhere?"

"Who said we're building anything?" He laughed. "Just keep reading."

Frowning, I did as he told me to and kept on reading. Apparently, the company had been hired to help perform an excavacation on some ancient structure that had been found in the middle of the jungle. It'd be an archeological job, then. Not my usual cup of tea, but digging stuff up was always fun. I just didn't understand why someone would pour money into such a thing when almost every single city across the continent needed the funds for rebuilding.

"You'll be in charge of operations there," Albernon continued once he realized I was through with the document. "You'll have to respect archeological procedures and whatnot, but aside from that, you'll have the reins."

"Alright, I'll get it done," I nodded. "Do you have any more information on it? Or should I just get there and start digging it all up?"

"Well, not exactly," he hesitated, scratching his chin. He looked around his desk and, once he found the document he was looking for, he pushed it into my hands. "That was drafted by Dr. Maki, the archaeologist on site. Those are her instructions."

"I see," I whispered as I skimmed the document. It seemed that Maki didn't really want me to dig the structure up, but to excavate the front of it so that a team could get inside and explore. It wouldn't be as fun as digging the whole thing up, but I didn't mind it.

What the archaeologist wanted me to do was a challenging thing, and I was always down for a challenge. "When am I leaving?"

"Today," he replied. "Is that a problem?"

"I rather just get started." Reaching across the desk, I grabbed one of Albernon's pens and a white piece of paper.

I bit the end of the pen for a couple of seconds as I thought, and then scribbled down all the machinery and material I would need for the job. Once I was done, I returned Albernon his pen and paper. "You think you can get me all that?"

"Sure," he nodded, and that without even looking at my notes. "Whatever you need, Alessa."

"I might ask you for some extra stuff once I get on site," I continued. "It'll be easier to know what I'm dealing with once I'm on the ground."

"I trust you," he shrugged. "Just tell me what you'll need, and I'll make sure it happens."

"Well…"

"I know, I know," he sighed. Pursing his lips, he leaned back in his chair and drummed his fingers against the tabletop once more. "You'll have an all human team with you, Alessa. But we can't screw this up. If things aren't working with them, I'll have you working with an alien crew again."

"Thank you," I breathed out, the relief evident in my voice. "I really appreciate it."

"Yeah, don't thank me just yet. This is a government job. These guys will pay us for our troubles, but they're expecting results. Drill that into everyone's skulls, alright? We need this contract to keep afloat for the time being."

"I won't disappoint you, you know that." Jumping up

to my feet, I offered him my hand. He shook it in that patient manner of his, and then gave me a smile.

"I was betting you'd say yes." His eyes crinkled with mischief. "You've never been one to stay idle. Your crew is already waiting for you in the city's hangar. I've rented a couple of transport shuttles to fly you all out there. The machinery and whatever else you requested will fly out tomorrow."

"Perfect, I'll get to it right away." Turning on my heels, I walked out of his office with a spring in my step. New projects always got me excited, and the fact that I would be back at work with an all-human crew just added to it. Rushing out of the building, I waved at a taxi and hopped inside it as fast as I could. I paid him extra so that he would wait for me as I packed for the trip and, just half an hour later, he was landing on the city's main hangar.

With my bag slung over one shoulder, I made my way toward the small fleet of transport shuttles docked there. I immediately recognized most of my old crew, and they all seemed pretty happy to see me.

Now I just hoped they wouldn't walk out on me. Construction jobs were always hard, but one happening in the middle of a jungle was bound to be extra hard.

While I enjoyed the challenge, most of these men were just looking for a steady paycheck.

"Alright, let's get to it, boys," I said out loud, pointing

at the shuttles. All of them start ambling toward the ships and, just fifteen minutes later, we were given clearance for takeoff.

Even though Albernon had booked me a seat on an executive shuttle, I took my place among the crew. To successfully run a construction crew, you have to show these men you don't think you're better than them.

No matter how many times we'd worked jobs together, it was a never ending dance.

"Try and get some sleep," I advised them. "It's going to be a long flight." Most of them acquiesced, closing their eyes and covering themselves with blankets the flight crew distributed. I tried to follow my own advice, but quickly gave up on it. Sleep never came easy before I had to start on a project.

Grabbing my briefcase, I retrieved all the documents and schematics I had been given and started going through them. I still had no idea why the government was this interested on an archaeological site, but I was starting to suspect there was more to this job than met the eye.

Even if on paper it seemed like someone was doing academic research through archaeological excavation, I was pretty sure there were other reasons for all this. What they were, though, I had absolutely no idea.

Only when my eyes started to burn did I look away

from the documents. I pinched the bridge of my nose and yawned, exhaustion seeping into my muscles.

Peering out the window, I smiled as I saw the edge of the jungle drawing close, the lush greenery of untouched lands always a sight to behold.

Stretching my back, I checked my watch and grabbed a blanket from under my seat, covering my legs with it. We were still one hour away from the site, which meant I could still get some shut eye before landing.

Still thinking of schematics and materials I would need to order, I drifted off to sleep.

NAVAT

"Looks like we're going to be here for a while," I said to the scientist. "Don't you think it's time we learn each other's names?"

"Why?" He said blankly. "I try not to acquire information I won't need."

His response caught me off guard.

I wasn't known for having the greatest manners on the planet, but surely, I was a step above this guy. He was downright unpleasant.

Before I could explain why knowing his name would be beneficial, an alert came in on my radio.

"Never mind," I shook my head. "I'll just call you Hey You from here on out."

I stepped away before he could respond.

"Navat," I announced into the radio.

"It's Axtin. I'm approaching the location."

Axtin? I assumed Dax or Amira would be coming out to the dig site.

"Great. You're cleared to enter. Watch out for the scientists," I cautioned.

"Why? Are they showing Gorgo signs?"

"No, they're just mean."

Axtin laughed into the radio before clicking off.

"Where should I set up?" A crisp, female voice caught my attention.

I turned around to find a human female standing close by with her hands on her hips.

Her eyes caught my attention before anything else. They looked like thunderclouds in both color and intensity. And her scent was enough to make my mind turn off.

"You're not Axtin," I blurted.

"What's Axtin?" She narrowed her eyes.

I blinked, forcing myself to focus.

"Who are you?" I asked. "I wasn't made aware of anyone else coming here."

"Should you have been?" She tilts her head to one side. "I'm Alessa Naro. I was called in to help excavate something. Do you have something in need of excavation?"

"Yes," I replied. "But I can't just let you walk in without clearance."

"I'm not sure I understand who you are." Her smile was tight and pointed.

"The feeling is mutual."

The tight smile turned into a scowl.

"Look," she sighed. "This isn't my usual gig, okay? My boss said someone called in for help and sent me."

"Who called in?" I asked.

"If you don't know, I'm not sure I should be disclosing that sort of information to you," she replied with a cold smirk.

"All I know is I'm authorized by General Rouhr and to be here. I would know if you had the same clearance," I said.

"Apparently, that's not true since you don't know who I am. Can you get out of my way now? I have a job to do."

She moved to step around me but I blocked her. I searched her eyes for any trace of a Gorgo but saw nothing. Still, something about her didn't sit right with me.

"I'm afraid I can't let you do that."

"Do I need to call someone?" she scowled at me. "Are you threatening me?"

"Are you Alessa?" Maki's voice came from behind me.

"Yes, I am. Do you know this oaf?"

"Oaf?" I sputtered.

"I see you've met Navat," Maki grinned. She stuck out her hand for Alessa to shake. Alessa smiled and looked instantly more at ease.

"Maki, can I speak to you for a moment?" I asked.

Maki gave me a confused look.

"Sure," she said after a moment of consideration.

I walked a few steps away and turned to Maki. I hoped I was out of her earsot, but this was important.

"You didn't mention calling in an external work team," I said.

"I was just on my way to tell you," Maki said. "I didn't expect her to get here this fast."

"Who is she?"

"She came highly recommended," Maki said. "She's worked with my cousin before. Very professional."

"She's an archaeologist?" I asked.

"No, she's actually a mechanical engineer," Maki supplied.

"Why do we need a mechanical engineer?"

"She can help us understand the structural integrity of what we're dealing with. The last thing we want is a cave in."

"I suppose," I said slowly.

Maki gave me a calculating look.

"What are you thinking?" She asked.

"Something about that woman is off," I said. "Have you verified everything about her?"

"No," Maki said slowly. "But she's well known in her field."

"I think we should talk to her more before allowing her into the dig site."

Maki furrowed her brow.

"What makes you say that?"

"When she approached, she refused to tell me who she was until I hounded her about it," I said. "And when you approached, her entire demeanor changed."

"Gorgo?"

"No," I shook my head. "Her eyes looked fine." Stunning, actually. But that wasn't the point.

"Then what?"

"Anti-alien."

Maki's eyes widened.

"No way," she gasped.

"Has she worked with any of General Rouhr's teams before?"

"Let me check." Maki pulled out her datapad and scrolled through Alessa's information. "No, she hasn't. Positions have been offered but she's turned them down."

"Interesting."

"Actually, her last team was replaced with soldiers from the *Vengeance* ground units," she said.

"Any notes on that?"

"Her boss left a comment," Maki said but didn't say anything more.

"Well?" I prompted.

"It says she's requested to only work with human teams in the future," Maki said in a small voice. She wouldn't make eye contact.

"That sounds anti-alien to me." I folded my arms across my chest.

"I'm not anti-alien," Alessa snapped from right behind me. "Those guys are psychotic."

"And I'm just supposed to take your word for it?"

"You don't have to take my word but you should take my credentials. How could I have such a high standing job if I was part of a radical faction?" She asked. "Before you say anything, take a look at my company's resume. They've done more than enough projects for Mayor Vidia and your General."

"She's right about that," Maki said. "Look."

Maki's datapad screen was filled with a list of projects her company and General Rouhr's team collaborated on, including Mayor Vidia's emergency housing buildings after the Puppet Master destroyed a section of buildings.

"Why would my company, who is not anti-alien in any way, hire me if I was anti-alien?" Alessa pressed.

"Answer me this," I looked at her with a level gaze. "What's your aversion to working with aliens?"

"It's not that I have an aversion, exactly" Alessa said quickly. "I was just pissy that my team walked out on me and that I had no say in who replaced them!"

"Why did they walk out?"

"We were working near Sauma," she explained. "Some of my guys got possessed, and the rest freaked out."

"You can't blame them for that." I furrowed my brow. "We still don't know what we're dealing with let alone how to counteract it."

"Yes, I realize that." Alessa stared daggers at me. "However, that didn't change the fact that we had a job to do and they left!"

"How does that tie into aliens?" I pressed.

"I don't think you understand the kind of trust it takes to work in a team like that," she said. "My boss replaced them all with strangers. Alien strangers. That didn't feel good."

"I don't think she's anti-alien, Navat," Maki sighed. "She hasn't called you scum yet."

"The day's not over," Alessa spat.

A smile tugged at the corner of my mouth. She had some fight in her. I liked that, even though this particular quality of hers had already proved to be a pain in my ass.

It'd been less than five minutes. That must be some kind of a record.

"I don't think she is either," I decided, ignoring the stunning female and going the reasonable route.

Talk to Maki only.

Srell.

Since when has agreeing with Maki been the reasonable route?

"I think she has an attitude problem but she's not a radical."

"An attitude problem?" Lightning flashed in Alessa's thundercloud eyes. "You're the one treating me like a criminal when I've done nothing wrong!"

"You refused to identify yourself at a classified site," I argued.

"How would I know the site existed if I wasn't privy to that information?" She demanded.

"If you had proper clearance, why didn't you just say so?"

"Because I didn't know who you were!"

"You don't have to know who I am. I have to know who you are."

"Is it really a mystery to you why I prefer to work with my own human team?" Alessa folded her arms across her chest.

"Okay, okay!" Maki stepped between us and held up her hands. "This sounds like a misunderstanding."

"I'll say," Alessa huffed.

"The two of you simply got off on the wrong foot,

that's all." Maki's smile was too big and too forced. "Let's start over, shall we?"

Neither Alessa or I moved to do anything.

Maki jabbed her elbow into my rib.

"I'm Navat of Strike Team Three," I recited unenthusiastically.

"Alessa Nora, mechanical engineer and not a species-ist."

"Could've fooled me," I growled.

"Enough," Maki let out an exasperated sigh. "For the sake of my sanity, let's get this project underway."

"You'll hear no argument from me," I muttered.

"Really? All I've heard from you are arguments," Alessa replied.

Maki stopped and looked up at the canopy.

"Today's going to be a long day," she said.

I couldn't have agreed more.

ALESSA

"Kill the engines," I cried out at the top of my lungs. The man piloting the excavator couldn't hear me, so I simply ran beside the hulking machine and stepped in front of it, waving my arms like a maniac. "Kill the goddamn engines!"

That did it.

The roaring sound of the engines finally subsided, and the pilot climbed out from the excavator's cabin with a confused look on his face. Taking his helmet off, he wiped the sweat off his brow with the back of his hand and made his way toward me.

"Anything wrong, boss?"

"No," I smiled, my heart still beating fast. "But according to the scans we're closing in on the entrance structure. We gotta stop using the excavator. We don't wanna risk the whole thing collapsing as we keep on moving dirt."

"Alright, I got it," he nodded. "So what now? Good ol' fashioned shovels?"

"That's right. Tameron is already debriefing the rest of the crew." Pointing toward a large canvas tent that had been set up a hundred yards behind the excavation site, I sent him on his way.

He walked away promptly, and I just studied the massive hole we had already dug.

Six days of digging, and we had moved nearly a million cubic feet of dirt. We could've gone way faster but, taking into account we had to be extra careful with the buried structure underneath, I was happy with the pace we were keeping.

If the schematics I had been handed were right, we were merely hours away from uncovering an entrance.

"What do you think?" I heard Maki say from behind me, and I spun around to find her looking at the hole, just like I was doing. "How long till we can get inside it?"

"A couple of hours more and we'll dig out the entrance," I replied. "That doesn't mean you'll be able to get inside it. Depending on the structure's state, we might have to build some ancillary structures inside it for support, just so it doesn't collapse on top of your team."

"Seems fair," she whispered, more to herself than to me. She kept her eyes focused on the thin layer of dirt covering her coveted structure, her gaze fiery and passionate. There was a lot that could be said about Maki, but the main thing was that she took her job seriously. She was as passionate about it as I was about engineering.

"With some luck," I continued, laying one hand on her shoulder as we climbed out of the pit and back through the tents, "the structure will be just fine and you'll be able to get started in a few hours."

"Fingers crossed," she smiled. "I'm gonna start prepping my team, just in case."

"You do that. My guys are already on their way."

Looking over Maki's shoulder, I could already see more than thirty workers walking out from the tent and heading straight toward the excavation.

As they went, the three Valorni on site joined the humans, Navat leading them.

They were all carrying heavy-looking shovels, far bigger than anything a regular human being could handle.

"Where do you think you're going?" I asked Navat the moment he passed me.

My tone was more sass than anything, and I hoped he'd pick up on that. Despite the fact that he was a Valorni, I actually liked the guy.

Maybe more than I should.

"I heard your foreman speak to your crew," he responded in that deep tone of his. I felt a shiver run up my spine, but I tried to ignore it. My body always reacted like this whenever I was close to him. "I figured you could use the help."

A smile spread across his lips, and he looked straight into my eyes. That was enough for my heart to start beating slightly faster.

"And do you think your guys are up to the task?" I teased him.

I knew that all of his men were competent workers, but I just couldn't resist poking him. Navat knew a lot about construction and excavation, probably more than I did in some fields, and maybe I could extend him the benefit of the doubt in this instance.

I was actually impressed that a soldier like him would be so knowledgeable, and I had been happy to accept his help during these past six days of excavations.

"Are you seriously asking me that?" Cocking one eyebrow up, he placed the spade of his shovel on the dirt and rested both hands on the handle, his eyes never leaving mine. "I thought you were smart."

"This isn't a job for the faint of heart," I said to Navat as I began to walk through the excavation tents. "We're doing sensitive work that's also hard."

"I've fought a war my whole adult life and had to deal with sensitive creatures like humans, so I can handle hard and sensitive work," Navat grunted.

I turned to look at him, fire in my eyes. I realized that we were alone, away from the main crowd of workers. We were behind a tent.

Tingles of electricity went up my spine. This was a perfect place if I was so inclined to...

No.

I needed to keep my head in the game. I struggled to remember what I was thinking.

"You think humans are fragile and sensitive?" I asked him. "After what we put up with the Xathi and now these possessed?"

"My crew did most of the fighting," Navat grinned as he retorted back. "And then we had to put up with the whiny humans who seemed to always complain and then go all anti-alien."

"Well maybe they have a point?"

"What point could they possibly have?"

"All you big giant sexy aliens came and destroyed our way of life and--"

"Wait. Big sexy aliens?" Navat asked. There was a grin on his face I wanted to slap off.

Or lick off.

"You know what I mean," I sputtered. "With big muscles and abs."

"Well, dainty little human woman, I think if you didn't like what you see then you'd--"

I didn't let him finish. Just talking to him was keying me up so much I couldn't think straight. It was like I was drunk. I reached up to him and got on my tiptoes and brought his head down to mine.

His mouth was eager and his tongue slipped into my mouth as he began massaging it.

I moaned.

The back of my brain screamed at me to stop. It kept telling me anyone could walk by at any point.

But Navat's hand went lower and I could feel his powerful hand grope my ass. I wanted him to squeeze it harder.

And he did.

This was heaven.

But it had to stop.

I broke free, with much reluctance.

Navat stood there, looking at me, a confused grin on his face.

"Looks like you're not so anti-alien after all," he said wryly.

"Alright, alright," I laughed, punching his massive shoulder. The moment my fingers touched his skin, I felt electricity crackle under my fingertips.

I hated the fact that my body reacted like this every

single time he was near, but I just couldn't seem to control it no matter how hard I tried.

Truth be told, I didn't try very hard. "Let's get to it, shall we? Maki is anxious to get started."

With a nod, Navat strode off, shovel over his shoulder, long strides eating up the distance to the excavation.

He started the descent into the hole we had dug, his boots kicking up dust as he went, and my eyes followed him.

"You like the guy, don't you?" Tameron asked me, and I spun on my heels to find him staring at me with an amused expression. "I can see it."

"Of course I don't like him," I sputtered, even though I already felt warm blood rush to my cheeks. "He just knows what he's doing. I respect that."

It sounded like a complete lie, but that was the best that I had to offer. No matter how much I trusted my foreman, I wasn't about to tell him that I felt attracted to Navat. After all, I didn't even know if I was *really* attracted to him.

If he was human, sure, he had all the qualities that I appreciated in a man...but he wasn't a human, was he? He was a Valorni, and I sure as hell wasn't going to fall for one of them.

That wouldn't be safe, or prudent.

"Whatever you say, Alessa," Tameron laughed, and

then he joined the masses of workers as they used their shovels and pickaxes to clear the dirt and rubble covering the structure's entrance. I remained atop of the clearing, checking on their progress with my wrist computer. According to the schematics, we were only a few feet away from—

"I think I hit something," one of the workers shouted, and that was enough for all the other workers to stop.

Before I thought things through, I threw myself onto the hole and rushed down the steep incline of dirt, only stopping once I was side by side with the man that had shouted.

Taking his shovel from his hands, I used the edge to clear the bits of dirt covering what seemed like a massive stone arch that led into a tunnel.

"Holy shit," I whispered. "We found it."

Taking a moment to catch my breath, I then ordered the rest of the workers to be as careful as they could as they opened the entrance up.

I still had to check the integrity of the entire thing, but I couldn't wait to go and break the news to Maki.

She was going to be over the moon.

I was climbing back up the hole when I heard screams coming from our campsite.

I rushed up, anxious to see what was going on, but I didn't have time to get all the way to the edge.

It only took a couple of seconds before Maki and her team of archaeologists jumped over the edge of the hole, all of them panicking as they rushed toward the excavation workers.

"What the hell's going on?" I cried out, grabbing Maki by the shoulder.

She turned around fast, her eyes wide with fear, and blinked twice before she realized who was talking to her. "Talk to me, Maki. What's going on?"

"The possessed," she breathed out, her words coated with fear. "They're here."

She had barely finished speaking when I started hearing the snarling of furious creatures just a few yards away from where I was.

Fighting against my instincts to run, I poked my head over the edge of the hole and my heart tightened as I saw a mass of bodies rush through the campsite.

I immediately recognized some of the workers from the Sauma bridge and, even though they still looked like humans, there was something beastly about them.

In their eyes, there was murder.

"What do we, Alessa?" Maki asked, tugging on the sleeve of my shirt. "What do we do?"

"I don't know," I replied, barely believing what I was seeing. "Half my guys are up there." My chest tightened. "Tameron-"

I was cut short by a pair of hands that latched

themselves to my throat. I rolled down the incline of dirt, a heavy body on top of me, and I found bloodshot eyes looking straight into mine.

One of the possessed had managed to get their hands on me.

I was as good as dead.

Except I wasn't.

The head of the hybrid sitting atop my chest snapped back as Navat hit him with his shovel, its snarl replaced by the nauseating sound of a neck being broken.

"Quick," Navat said, grabbing me by the wrist and pulling me up to my feet. "We gotta get inside!"

I didn't complain.

I just let him drag me inside the structure, the ancient shadows of millennia ago wrapping themselves around us.

It wasn't a safe thing to do, but right now safety was just a detail.

Our lives were on the line.

NAVAT

"Go, go, go!" I shouted.

I looked around at the wounded. Some were able to get up and move, others sustained too many injuries.

"I'm sorry," I whispered to them, even though they couldn't hear me. Some were already gone.

Maki knelt beside one of the excavation workers. She pumped their chest in an attempt to start their heart. It didn't work.

I forced myself to look away.

I grabbed Maki by the shoulder and shoved her in front of me.

"Go!" I urged again.

"Where am I going?" She shrieked.

"Anywhere. Away from here," I directed. I gave

Tyehn a push in Maki's direction. "Cover her," I told him.

"What if there are more hostiles?" Maki called back to me.

"Just go!"

I didn't stop to watch them run off. I started grabbing everyone in sight and pushing them in the direction of the tunnel.

A Gorgo infested human ran up on me. I fired one shot off the stun gun and it fell to the ground, quivering.

"Good call on the stun guns, Maki," I muttered to myself.

"Give me one of those!" I whirled to see Alessa standing beside me.

"I told you to run!"

"I'm not leaving until everyone else is safe first," she protested. "I always take care of my team."

Her voice cracked on the last word. Even as Gorgo infested humans closed in around us, I was impressed.

"Focus on helping those who can still be helped," I told her.

She looked back to the unlucky ones, dead or dying on the ground.

She nodded once. She understood.

She stayed near me as we pushed people towards

shelter. Once we had everyone else pointed in the right direction, I ushered her into the darkness.

"Who's covering you?" She called back to me.

"The stun gun."

"How many shots does that little sucker have?" She forced a light tone into her voice, likely to distract herself from the horrors unfolding around her.

"Great question. I'm sure we'll find out soon."

"Very funny."

"I'm not kidding. I've never used one of these in a practical situation."

A shrieking growl cut me off. I whirled around and threw a blind punch in the darkness. My fist connected with a jaw.

The shrieking stopped but I knew more of the infected were coming after us. A snarl on my left startled me. I hadn't heard it approach.

"Oh, no you don't," Alessa grunted. I looked at her just in time to see her leg come up and make contact with the jaw of an infected human.

"Nice kick," I said.

"I take it that means thank you."

"Something like that."

We took off after the others, stopping periodically to stun, punch, or kick the infected as they came after us.

We took several sharp turns. I couldn't tell if we

were entering tunnel offshoots or if the corridor simply turned. I hoped someone ahead of us knew where we were going because I sure as hell didn't.

"It looks like this access shaft is getting narrower," Alessa observed.

"Is that a good or a bad thing."

"Good because less infected can come after us," she said. "Bad because narrow shafts tend to lead to dead ends."

"I hope you're wrong."

"I hope your stun gun doesn't run out of rounds."

"Is there someone in front of you within calling distance?" I asked.

"Yeah, why?"

"Tell them to pass a message along to Maki. I want her stun gun."

"Don't you have any other weapons?" I could hear the indignation in her voice even though I couldn't see the look on her face.

"Of course," I tutted. "However, I don't want to use deadly force if I don't have to. Our goal is to remove the Gorgo infection from humans, not kill them."

"Right," Alessa said softly. "When they're attacking like this, it's easy to forget they're still human. Apologies."

"Don't apologize to me," I said. "Apologize to them

for kicking them in the face when we get the Gorgo out of them."

"Will do." I heard the smile in her voice even though I couldn't see it.

Alessa passed on my message to the person in front of her. I could only assume the person carried it forward.

"It's like telephone," Alessa mused.

"A telephone?"

"No, telephone. The game. One person whispers a phrase to another," Alessa paused to drive her fist into the nose of an infected. "The phrase gets passed from person to person and at the end, you see how much the phrase was altered."

"This phrase needs to remain unaltered," I said.

"I know but this is a stressful situation so let me make this fun, okay?" Alessa huffed.

"You don't think punching hostiles is fun?" I smirked.

"What happened to 'these are still humans', huh?" She shot back.

"I let you have your telephone fun. Let me have mine."

I whirled around and fired a stun shot at an infected just three feet away from me.

We'd moved so deep into the underground structure that no natural light penetrated the tunnel anymore.

The only light sources were the lighted helmets some of the excavation team wore and the lights from our tech.

"Hide your lights," I urged Alessa. "We're glowing targets. Pass it forward. Everyone in the back half of the group should try to go dark."

"Kill your lights," Alessa shouted to the person ahead of us.

I didn't have a headlamp, but there were small lights on my radio and comm unit. I did my best to tuck them under my clothing.

I watched as the frantic herd of scientists and excavators dimmed their lights. The front portion of the group stayed illuminated.

I could see where Maki and Tyehn were leading the way. Hopefully, they wouldn't run us into a dead end.

The light trick worked. Somewhat.

The infected pushed forward, trying to get to the illuminated people at the head of the group. This led to them crashing into me frequently.

Inconvenient, but at least I could take them by surprise. I never struck them with my full strength. I didn't want to do permanent damage, I just wanted to knock them out.

"Here's Maki's stun gun." Alessa pressed a second stunner into my hand.

"Excellent," I grinned.

"We have a problem!" Maki's shrill voice carried all the way to the back of the group where Alessa and I were.

"What kind of problem?" Alessa's voice was pinched with fear. So far, she'd done a great job at hiding her terror. I hoped she'd be able to hold it together, at least a little longer.

"I don't know where to go!"

"Keep moving," I urged Alessa, keeping one hand on her shoulder to guide her and the other pointing the stun gun into the darkness behind us.

Even if there was a dead end ahead, we couldn't stop.

Not here.

One of the possessed shrieked. I fired a stun round in the direction of the noise and was rewarded with the sound of the stun dart striking something fleshy.

The group spilled into a brightly lit circular chamber.

High above us was a perfect circle of natural light, though it was far too high for us to climb through even if we stood on each other's shoulders.

I spied a few archways leading to other parts of the structure, but they were filled to the brim with rubble.

There was no way out, not in the time we had.

"What do we do?" Alessa whispered to me.

The group moved away from the opening of the tunnel as the possessed started pouring in.

I fired the stun gun until it was empty, then I emptied Maki's but the possessed kept coming.

"Not too many rounds in those little things, huh?" Alessa quipped in a wavering voice.

"Not as many as I'd like," I replied.

"Tell me you have a plan B," she said.

"I do but I was hoping not to use it."

"That's why it's called a plan B."

"Tyehn! Axtin!" I shouted.

They appeared at my side.

"Do you have any stun shots left?"

"Only a few," Tyehn replied. Another wave of the infected came through. Tyehn lifted his stun gun and fired off the last of his rounds. "Never mind."

"Axtin?"

"I only have lethal weapons," he replied.

"Right," I nodded. "Any close combat weapons?"

"A utility knife." Axtin took a short, thick blade from his belt just in time to drive it into the shoulder of an infected that got too close. It reeled back, screeching in pain. Blood gushed from the wound. I wasn't an expert in human blood but something about the infected's blood looked wrong. It looked too thick.

"We're going to have to resort to lethal measures," I said.

"I know," Tyehn nodded. "I don't like it but it's them or us at this point."

"Everyone, stay back!" Axtin ordered as if they weren't already cowering against the far wall. Alessa stood beside Maki at the front of the group, her stormy eyes wildly darting about.

I pulled a blaster from my belt. The others did the same. We took positions in the center of the room and waited for more of the infected to come through.

When they did, we put them down quickly.

It was hard to determine whether we shot through all of them or if remaining infected understood the danger and decided against attacking us.

I almost hoped it was the former. I didn't want the fleeing infected to circle back around and attack us later on.

"What's it doing?" Alessa cried out. I followed her gaze to an infected that was frantically tearing at the supports of the archway we just came through.

"Take him down!" I ordered.

Axtin and Tyehn fired at the infected. He crumpled to the ground but not after seriously damaging the structural integrity of the archway.

The infected stopped attacking after that, retreating back down the tunnel.

After a beat of silence, I lowered my weapon.

"Is everyone all right?" I asked everyone but I found

my gaze drawn to Alessa in particular. She gave me a curt nod.

"I don't think we're going out the way we came in." Maki walked over to the damaged archway. She took one step too close and it started crumbling even more.

"What's the plan?" Axtin asked no one in particular.

"Get out," Alessa replied.

"Sounds good. Which way?"

All of us stopped and looked around. It quickly became abundantly clear that no one had any clue where we were within the structure that Fen had scanned.

All of the archways leading from the chamber were blocked with rubbled.

We were lost.

ALESSA

It was hell.

We had no idea where we were, there was a murderous horde of alien hybrids looking for us, and a lot of the survivors were injured.

What was supposed to be nothing but a simple engineering operation, had now turned into a complete disaster.

The rest of my team that had been on the surface...Tameron.

They were gone.

They had to be.

I couldn't think about them. I'd mourn them later.

If there was a later.

Still breathing hard, I looked down at my hands to

find them covered with blood. It wasn't my own, that much I knew, but that didn't relieve me.

If anything, it just made me feel more concerned. I thought that by enlisting my human crew I was doing the guys a favor, but as it turned out I had just dragged them all here to be slaughtered.

"Oh, God, it hurts," a man sobbed beside me, and I pursed my lips as I looked down at him. He was crouched against the wall, clutching an arm that seemed to be angled in a way that wasn't natural. Going down on one knee, I whispered a few words of comfort as I tried to assess the damage.

"Your arm's broken," I muttered, not knowing what else to say. "Try not to move it too much." My words were useless—he was in pain, of course he wasn't going to be waving his arm around—but it helped to say something.

Looking around me, though, I quickly realized that I'd take more than just words to get out of this situation.

Most of the men were sporting wounds—thankfully most of them were just bruises, scratches and cuts—and the morale was as low as I had ever seen it.

"How are you?" Navat asked me.

I went up to my feet and looked at him, having no idea on how to reply. His shirt was ragged and covered in blood, and his knuckles were bruised. He no longer looked like a construction man, but like a soldier. I hated that, all the killing and violence, but I couldn't blame him for it. Navat and his men hadn't wanted to kill, but they had had no choice. If they hadn't done what they did, there'd be no survivors right now.

"I don't know," I said as I shook my head. "I really don't know." My voice sounded weak and frail, like brittle glass. "What are we going to do now?"

"We'll figure something out," he replied, and he sounded so certain of it that I almost believed him.

The sobs of the wounded men all around me, though, kept me grounded in reality. I looked down at my mud-caked boots for a second, but Navat reached for me and placed two fingers under my chin.

Forcing me to look up and into his eyes, he offered me a smile. "We'll figure something out, Alessa," he repeated, and this time I found myself nodding at his words.

"But what exactly?"

"Do you still have your wrist unit?" He asked, and I raised my arm almost immediately. Although the screen was cracked and covered with dirt, the tiny computer on my wrist seemed to be fully operational. It lit up as I tapped it with one finger, and I quickly wiped the dirt covering its screen.

"Good thinking," I whispered, moving my fingers across the screen while I looked for the schematics of the place. We'd only have sonar scans and satellite imagery to go by, which weren't exactly a map, but it was better than nothing. "Oh, crap."

"What's wrong?"

"Either the unit's damaged, or somehow the files have become corrupted," I pushed past gritted teeth, not even looking away from the screen. "See? I can open the schematics, but only for seconds at a time. It's useless."

"Let me see," he said in a comforting tone, and I quickly unstrapped the unit from my wrist and handed it to him. "Well, it's not much, but it's something. I think we can use it for navigation. It's the only shot we have right now, anyway."

Carefully, he took one step toward me and strapped the unit back on my wrist, his fingers gently brushing against the skin on my forearm. I held my breath as he did it, his touch making me feel things I couldn't quite process.

At least not right now, lost and trapped in some ancient maze.

"What are you guys doing?" Walking up to us, Maki ran one hand through her disheveled hair and sighed heavily.

She seemed slightly disoriented, pieces of dirt covering her shoulders and arms, but was otherwise okay. "Is your unit working? If it is, maybe we can use the schematics and—"

"We're on it already," I said, offering her a quick smile. "They don't work as well as I'd like them to, but we'll figure something out."

From the corner of my eye, I noticed Navat smiling. Even if unconsciously and just to reassure Maki, I had used his words. I just hoped he was right and that, in the end, we'd truly figure something out.

"If you guys say so," Maki whispered. She blew a lock of hair away from her face, and then shook her head. "You know, I thought I'd be happy to get inside this place, but now I can't wait to get out."

"Yeah, no one imagined we'd get in like this," I said.

"It's not just that," Maki continued. "This place just...I don't know how else to put it, but it seems all wrong. Can't you guys smell it? There's this weird mustiness in the air. A place this ancient wouldn't smell like this. It's just—"

She trailed off the moment a few men raised their voices behind us. We all turned around to see what the commotion was, but it was hard to see anything in the dark tunnel we were in. The only lights we had came from the lanterns attached to the workers' helmets, and they struggled to keep the shadows at bay.

"What's going on back there?" I asked, pushing my way past a group of men. I narrowed my eyes as I saw a couple of men pinning another one against the wall, and I immediately rushed toward them. We couldn't afford to start fighting among each other if we wanted to make it out of his place alive. "Stop it, the three of you! What the hell do you think you're doing?"

"We can't," one of the men hissed, and only when I drew close did I realize why he wouldn't let go. The man they had pinned against the wall seemed to be having some sort of low-key seizure, his eyes rolling in their sockets, and there was a bit of foam dripping down his chin.

It was a morbid scene, but it was about to get even worse.

Without any sudden warning, the man's body relaxed and he stood straight. His eyes rolled once more, except this time they returned to their natural position. Except they weren't the eyes of a sane man. Hell, they weren't even the eyes of a man. There was an alien madness living there, one that made my stomach lurch.

Taken by surprise, the two men that had been grabbing him jumped back, and a sadistic grin immediately took over his lips.

Before anyone could stop him, he pushed his way past the two men and launched himself down the dark tunnel, the shadows welcoming him almost too eagerly.

"The hosts," I heard him snarl in the distance, his voice bouncing off the ancient walls like a threat. "Have to find the hosts." He continued to speak, but by then he was already too far for me to make out the exact words.

"What the hell just happened?" Maki asked me, her words just a frail little whisper. She had gone pale too, and her hands were trembling. "Did he…?"

"Yeah," I nodded. "He just turned."

"Should we go after him or do anything?"

"I'll send an alert to look out for him to all teams, but there's nothing we can do right now."

None of us said a word, the realization that we were no longer safe inside this structure dawning on us. Suddenly, this place didn't seem like shelter. It seemed like a very dark, very cold tomb.

I turned around to find Navat standing behind the two of us. There was a seriousness etched deep in his face, and his fists were clenched.

Once more, he was ready to spill blood to keep us safe. And thank God for that. With him around, there was still hope..

"What do we do?" I asked him, fully knowing we'd have to rely on his skills to escape this place.

But this time, not the ones I'd seen in the last six days.

Now I needed his skills as a soldier.

"We do as we planned," he said, "and we get the hell out of here."

NAVAT

"Can you walk?" I asked my annoying scientist friend whose name I still didn't know.

"Yeah," he gave a shaky nod. "What's going to happen to that guy? The one that started talking about hosts?"

"I don't know yet," I replied. "We don't have the manpower to protect the group and track him down. If he doesn't bother us, we won't bother him."

"That doesn't seem like a smart plan," he said.

"Got a better one?" Alessa piped up. I looked over my shoulder to find her standing a few yards behind me.

She looked a little lost and unsure of herself. The blood on her hands dried and had started crumbling away, leaving behind a stain.

My first instinct was to find a way for her to wash her hands but I knew we didn't have that option. Any water we had on hand needed to be conserved in case we couldn't find a way out right away.

"No," the scientist replied, looking away.

"Then let us worry about it." Alessa's voice took on a gentler tone. The scientist offered a faint smile but didn't look our way again.

"Do you have a plan?" Alessa asked me as we walked away from the huddled survivors.

"Several," I said. "However, none of them are full plans and they require a fair amount of good luck to make them happen."

"So, basically, all of your plans are half baked fantasies," she said.

"Exactly. Just don't tell anyone." I winked at her.

She shook her head and rolled her eyes. At least she wasn't in a catatonic state like some of the others. If I kept her talking and moving, she'd probably be okay.

"We should move on," Axtin said. "The Gorgos know we're here. There's nothing stopping them from coming back and tearing into us all over again."

"Maybe avoid phrases like 'tearing into us' around the traumatized survivors, yeah?" Maki admonished.

"Sorry," Axtin shrugged. "But I'm right."

"I'm hoping that precarious archway will keep them at bay while we figure this out," Alessa said. "We have to clear the rubble from the other archways but there's no telling where they'll lead."

"Open your map, if you can." I urged.

She lifted her wrist and pulled up the map. It shone brightly before flickering out just as it had been doing before.

"Did you see anything?" I asked her.

She gave me a blank look.

"You're kidding right?"

"It's all we have. Look at it and try to figure out if one archway is better than the others."

A few minutes and several frustrated sighs later, Alessa lowered her wrist.

"There are no guarantees here, so if I'm wrong, don't get mad at me," she started. "But if we clear out the west arch, I think we'll have a decent chance of getting somewhere other than here."

"Like outside?" Axtin asked.

"If we're lucky." She looked at me from the corner of her eye. I smirked.

Alessa, Axtin, Tyehn, Maki and I approached the western arch.

"How do you propose we do this?" I asked.

"Don't lift from the bottom and don't lift with your back," Alessa said.

"That's all the words of wisdom we get?" Axtin asked.

"That, and give me a boost?" Alessa looked over her shoulder and grinned. She was trying to seem unbothered by the injured survivors. I knew how badly she was shaken, but I wasn't about to call her on it. She was learning how to cope with this sort of thing. That was good. She needed it.

"Navat, give her a boost," Axtin said to me.

"Pretty sure she asked you," I replied.

"Right but I can lift more than you," he countered.

"That's pure skrell," I snorted. "But, to prove I'm the better individual, I'll give you a boost, Alessa."

"Men," Maki rolled her eyes.

"I made a mistake in thinking alien and human males were so different," Alessa sighed. She looked somewhat less tense than she had a moment ago.

Good.

Making her laugh would've been nice, but giving her a chance to mock me would take her mind off of what we'd just endured.

I wasn't sure why her state of mind mattered so much to me. I tried to tell myself that I needed her to be sharp for the sake of the team and nothing more.

Couldn't lie to myself, though. Something about Alessa intrigued me, even if every time we spoke we ended up arguing.

Or I wanted to tear her clothing off...

That kiss confused the srell out of me.

The idea of her being in distress over what she witnessed gave me a bad feeling.

I knelt down, gesturing to Alessa to step on my interlocked fingers.

"Tyehn, give me a boost as well?" Maki asked.

"You got it."

Tyehn knelt down as I had done.

"I'll take the rubble," Axtin said.

Alessa and Maki began pulling out chunks of ruin and debris with as much care as they could manage. They passed pieces to Axtin so he could pile them up someplace out of the way. He helped dislodge larger pieces as well, the ones that were too big for both Alessa and Maki to lift.

"The archway looks structurally sound," Alessa said after a moment of consideration. She was standing on her own two feet now. We'd cleared away most of the rubble. There was enough room for someone to step through.

A chilling laugh caught my attention. It was faint. I didn't think the others heard it but it was certainly there.

"Did you hear that?"

"Hear what?"

"Listen," I urge.

We fell silent. I stared into the darkness, straining against the soft moans and murmurs.

The laugh came again, a slow cackling.

"That sounds like the Gorgo," Maki whispered.

"But he ran through the other arch," Axtin said.

"Then that means there's a way out," Alessa murmured. "If the Gorgo came around this way, that means there's another structurally sound set of corridors somewhere in here."

"That's swell and all, but that also means the Gorgo can hunt us down here," Axtin pointed out.

"I'd rather be moving target than sitting bait," Tyehn said.

"Agreed," I nodded.

"We'll have to do something about the Gorgo eventually," Maki said.

"We should let him live for as long as we can," I suggested.

"What?" Alessa snapped. "Why? You saw him! He's rabid."

"Because we've never gotten to see a transformation, for lack of a better word," I said. "We can see the stages of it, the early signs, the progression. We might witness something that could eventually lead us to a cure."

"That's so sentimental of you," Maki beamed.

"It's not sentiment, it's practicality," I corrected.

"It's a little bit of both," Tyehn said.

"Fine," I grumbled.

"What's wrong with being sentimental?" Alessa asked me.

The question caught me off guard.

"I," I stammered.

"That wasn't meant to be a brain teaser," Alessa smiled.

"I suppose it's because so few things in life are permanent," I said. "Getting too attached detracts focus from the necessary things. The permanent things."

"That's fair, I suppose," Alessa nodded.

"A little bleak," Maki added.

"Is now really the time to cross-examine my personal philosophies?" I barked.

"If it stops me from thinking about what a shit situation, we're in, yes," Alessa said.

I clicked my tongue.

"Unfortunately, we need to get these survivors moving out of this shit situation so let's get it done."

Luckily, none of the survivors had any severe injurics preventing them from walking. There was a sprained ankle or two among the group, maybe a broken arm, but all in all, we were in good shape.

All considered.

"You want to take the lead on this one?" Maki asked. "I'm a little burnt out on leading after blindly careening through the darkness."

"Sure," I smirked.

"I'll help," Alessa offered. "We can use my map for a few seconds every once in a while."

"That's better than nothing," I chuckled.

"I'll take the end of the pack," Axtin said. "If anything sneaks up behind us, I'll take them down."

I nodded.

"Tyehn and I will float up and down the line. We'll make sure no one shows signs of an unwelcome Gorgo visitor."

We took our positions in front of the newly cleared archway. Alessa opened her map for a split second.

"If we head southeast, we'll be sort of in the right direction," she said.

"Is sort of the best we can do?"

"For now, yes," she said.

"All right. Let's get doing."

I kept my weapon tucked away but had my hand hovering over the hilt, ready to grab at a moment's notice.

"I bet crazy things happen at all your job sites," I said lightly.

Alessa smirked faintly but said nothing.

"You handled all of that really well," I said. "I'm impressed and there isn't much that impresses me."

"Thanks," she said, voice flat.

I wondered if she was entering into shock. Sometimes it took a moment to kick in.

"If you want to make a joke about not working with aliens ever again, now would be the time," I said.

"I'll take you up on that at some point," she said.

She powered up her map and let it flicker.

"Still southeast?"

"For a little while. Eventually, we'll reach a turn."

I said nothing. Instead, I focused on listening for the laughter of the Gorgo.

Everything would be fine once we got out of here.

ALESSA

I understood what he was trying to do. If I wasn't so fucking freaked out right now, I might have appreciated it. Maybe it was an alien thing, maybe it was a guy thing. Either way, he was completely oblivious to the fact that I wanted to be left alone to wrestle with my temper.

I appreciated all of the witty banter designed to take my mind off of the injured people who I was supposed to keep safe.

It had worked for a little while. It wasn't working anymore.

I didn't want to say anything. Within five minutes of meeting Navat, I had pegged him as an asshole.

Perhaps, I wasn't totally correct. He was an asshole,

but a nice asshole. An asshole with a heart of gold, if I may.

Over the last six days, he'd taken every bit of discomfort I had with working with aliens, and turned it into an entirely different kind of discomfort.

And I wasn't even going to think about that kiss...

I took a moment to be thankful for the fact that telepathy wasn't a thing. If anyone around me was listening in on my thoughts, they'd think I was a crazy person. I was just attacked by a mob of Gorgo infested humans.

I was allowed to have a few crazy thoughts bouncing around in my brain.

I refused to look at my hands. I never got the chance to rinse the blood off. I didn't want to see what color my skin was stained. I could almost feel it on my skin as if it was a living thing. I wanted to scratch it off, skin and all.

No, I couldn't lose my cool here. Once I was outside again, once I could feel the sun again, then I'd freak out. It would be my reward for surviving this mess.

My boss was going to get an earful next time he sees me. I'm going to demand a raise. I'm going to demand a better retirement plan. I'm definitely going to demand the right to refuse jobs.

I wasn't even supposed to be here!

I wasn't hired by my company to be an excavator or archeologist.

But I'd happily taken the job.

"Are you all right?" Navat asked in a gentle voice that sounded like nails on a chalkboard to me. No, that wasn't fair. He was just trying to be helpful. I shouldn't take my dangerously high temper out on him.

I just couldn't stop seeing the faces of the people back at the camp, the ones that didn't make it down into the structure.

Tameron.

All of them.

I should've been able to do something. Anything. But I couldn't. All I could do was run. I ran. I regretted it.

"Alessa?" He asked sharply.

I blinked and looked at him.

"Sorry, I was lost in thought," I said in a harsher tone than I should have.

"Just making sure you aren't slipping into shock. We need you," he said.

"I'll do my best."

Navat pulled me aside from the main group, and while I resisted at first, a part of me was thankful.

"It's going to be okay," he said in his deep voice.

"How can you be sure?" I asked, more fragile than I would have liked.

"Because I'll protect you," he said.

"And what if something happens to you?"

"Nothing will happen to me, Alessa," he said calmly and confidently. It gave me strength.

Without realizing what I was doing I rested my head on his broad chest. I could feel the breaths he was taking.

It was soothing. I could do that forever, I thought.

"Hey, what's that?" Maki called from her place in the middle of the group.

We turned to look. She'd stopped near the wall, pointing into a space that was slightly darker than the space around us. I'd been so lost in thought that I'd walked right by it.

Navat shined his light in the space. There was a small archway carved into the wall. It was taller and skinnier than the ones we'd walked through before.

The darkness beyond the archway devoured the light from Navat's flashlight.

Something stirred in my chest. I couldn't properly describe it. I was suddenly plagued with the deep need to see where that pathway lead.

"Do you think it's the way out?" Axtin asked.

"I think it has as good of a chance as being the way out as going straight has," Tyehn reasoned.

"I think we should go," Maki said with certainty. "It feels right."

"What?" Navat furrowed his strong brow.

"I can't explain it," Maki said. "I just feel like it's what we're supposed to do."

"I feel the same thing," I said.

Navat turned his quizzical gaze on me.

"All right," Axtin declared. "Let's go."

I made my way toward the opening with Maki. Tyehn and Navat followed behind us. The survivors murmured in confusion at the abrupt change in direction.

"Where does that lead?" A scrawny man asked. I didn't know his name but he really seemed to hate Navat.

Navat wasn't his biggest fan either. It was sort of amusing.

"We're going to find out," Navat said to him with an ear to ear grin. The sour expression on the scientist's face almost brought a smile to mine.

His gaze slid to mine. He caught me watching the exchange. He didn't say anything. He just winked.

I felt a smile pulling at the corners of my mouth.

Navat walked through the archway first. Even though my map wasn't working, I followed behind him anyway. From the scant images, I was able to glean from the flickering map, this corridor wasn't reflected anywhere.

That was a complete surprise, but maybe it shouldn't be.

I knew the satellite images were taken with Urai tech. As advanced as it was, I didn't believe it to be infallible.

At least, that's what I told myself.

That was less frightening than the alternative. That this particular corridor possessed some kind of cloaking technology capable of hiding it from advanced satellites.

We walked in silence. The corridor wasn't as long as I imagined it to be. We only walked for a few moments before the corridor opened up into a room. Unlike the other rooms we'd stumbled across, this one wasn't empty.

"What is that?" I gasped as my headlamp landed on a carefully placed object wrapped in dirty swaths of fabric.

"Please tell me it's not what I think it is," Maki whispered.

Navat stepped forward.

I didn't follow.

He shone his light on the object.

"It's a body."

I found myself scrambling back, embedding myself in the group of survivors.

"Human?" Tyehn asked.

"I don't think so," Navat replied. "Unless something was done to them."

Oh, that was an unsettling thing for him to say.

"Let me take a look," Axtin said. Navat and Tyehn gave him a look. "What? Leena's taught me about human physiology. I pay attention to my mate's work."

Leena sounded like a human. I heard rumors about the aliens taking human mates but I didn't know if they were true or not. I supposed they were.

Interesting.

Axtin stepped up to the wrapped object.

"Definitely not human," he said. "They look more like Urai than anything."

I crept closer to the alien men. Navat noticed me and stepped aside so I could have a better look.

Axtin was right. Whatever it was, it wasn't human. Most of its body was wrapped, but its face was left exposed to the elements. The arrangements of its facial features were human enough, in the sense that it had two ears, two eyes, a nose, and a mouth, but the comparisons stopped there. It was a long, skinny being of at least seven feet tall.

Parts of its skull were elongated, giving the effect of wearing a crown.

Very strange, indeed.

The area around it wasn't clean, but it was neatly

arranged. Rows of little pots lined the body. Dried flowers were placed around the head of the being.

"This is an altar," I whispered.

"Look," Maki said softly. "There are more."

She shone her light around the room. The walls were lined with altars just like the one we stood before.

"This is a tomb," Navat said.

"The rest of the structure doesn't support that theory," I mused. "Parts of this structure look modern. This is the oldest looking part I've seen so far."

"The mystery deepens," Axtin murmurs.

"Perhaps only this chamber was used for burials. The rest of the structure could've been used for other things," Tyehn said.

"That's possible," I agreed.

"Hey, guys," Maki said. "Look at this."

The beam of her light illuminated lines of unfamiliar characters on the wall.

"Anyone know what that says?" Axtin asked.

"I've never seen anything like it before," I said.

"Neither have I," Navat echoed.

"I wish I could document this," Maki sighed. "This is a significant find."

"I have a camera," I offered.

They all turned to look at me.

"When did you have time to grab a camera?" Navat asked me.

"I keep it clipped to my utility belt," I explained.

I unclipped my camera, which looked like nothing more than a thin black bar.

"It's not crystal-clear quality, but it'll pick up the writing." I passed it to Maki.

"Thanks," she smiled and snapped several photos.

"It looks like there's another room opposite of where we came in." Navat shone his flashlight in that direction, illuminating another tall, thin archway.

We moved as a group through the row of altars into the next chamber only to find more of the same.

"How many do you think there are?" Maki asked.

"Chambers or bodies?" I asked back.

"Either. Both," she replied.

"Wait a moment." Navat stopped walking. "Look at the writing in here."

He shone his light on the wall, illuminating more lines of script.

"That's not the same writing in the other room," I observed.

"There are pictures too," Axtin pointed out. "I can't tell what they're depicting."

Near the writing was a series of panels. The lines were most certainly deliberate but I didn't have a clue what the images represented.

Maki took more pictures.

"And look," Maki pointed straight ahead. "Another chamber."

"What is this?" I asked myself more than anyone else. No one answered. No one had a clue what we'd found.

We moved into the next chamber.

There were more altars, more bodied but different writing and pictures.

We found three more chambers after that.

The more we saw, the less we understood.

NAVAT

"This place is screwing with us," Axtin declared after we passed the same strange room for the third time.

Row after row of long narrow beds lined the walls.

At least these were unoccupied.

Not a corpse or a Gorgo in sight.

"Maybe this isn't the same room," Maki suggested.

"It's odd enough that there would be one room like that, let alone three," I said. "What would something like this be doing here in the first place? There's nothing around for miles."

"I have a theory about that," Alessa said. "I saw something in the last room, but didn't think it was important enough to stop moving for."

"What was it?"

"Bars slots for bars in the floor. As in, prison bars," she said.

"You think this was a prison?" Maki gave her a quizzical look.

"It could also have been a hospital," Alessa said. "I can't think of anything else that has rows of beds like that. Maybe a dormitory, but then where's the rest of the living quarters?"

"But what kind of hospital has bars?" Tyehn asked.

"Not a good kind," Alessa shuddered.

A rumble of laughter echoed through the corridors.

"Host. Host. Host." The Gorgo chirped.

The survivors heard it this time. They huddled together, murmuring frantically to one another.

"Everything's okay," Maki soothed. "We have weapons. General Rouhr trains his soldiers well."

"We've handled way worse," Axtin said with a dismissive wave.

A peal of laughter made Alessa jump beside me. Without thinking, I reached out and touched her arm. We both stared at my hand on her sleeve.

I expected her to twist away, but she stayed put.

After a moment, I dropped my hand. It was that, or pull her closer to me.

"Why is he laughing?" Maki wondered.

"Did you see him?" One of the survivors stuttered. "He's mad."

"But is he?" I said. "Did the Gorgo drive him mad? Is the Gorgo itself mad? We don't know."

"Not helpful," Alessa muttered to me.

"They asked," I replied.

"Why hasn't he attacked us?" Axtin wondered. "We all saw him transform."

"Either he knows we outgun him or the Gorgo doesn't have full control yet," I replied.

"Find them. Find them," a guttural voice came from the darkness.

"Can I please just shoot him?" Axtin asked through clenched teeth.

"It would be great if we could catch him," I said. "Take him back with us."

Maki and Alessa looked at me like I'd lost my mind.

"Leena and Dr. Parr need more test subjects," I shrugged. "This guy is a prime candidate. Besides, we might be able to help him if we get lucky."

"A good portion of our future depends on luck and I'm not thrilled with that," Alessa said.

"We're relying on pure luck to get us out of here, that's for sure," Axtin said.

"Let's get back to the building," Tyehn suggested. "Figuring it out might help us get out of here sooner."

"I had a thought," Alessa said. "It's along the line of unpleasant hospitals."

"A death ward?" I asked.

"An asylum."

"Oh," Maki said softly.

"It's a halfway mark between a prison and a hospital."

"Obviously another species built it," Tyehn reasoned. "Something that lived here before the humans did."

"It's possible," Maki said. "But we've never found signs of something being here so recently before us." She shook her head. "This isn't anywhere as old as the temple Amira found in the desert."

"A fair amount of your planet is unexplored," Axtin points out. "I wouldn't rule out yet another ancient civilization here."

"I don't want to think about that," Maki shuddered.

"Why not?" I asked.

"Every time we discover a new lifeform on the planet, things get hard for us," she explained.

Axtin, Tyehn and I exchanged glances.

"Are we supposed to be insulted by that?" Axtin asked.

"No," Maki shook her head. "Don't get me wrong, I'm so glad you're all here. But when the *Vengeance* crashed, life got harder for the humans. That's just facts."

"The Xathi were a shit show," Alessa said.

"The Puppet Master messed us up for a while,"

Maki added. "Though, I'm glad we have the Puppet Master now. Still doesn't change the destruction he caused."

"Now we have Gorgos," Alessa finished. "They aren't making things any easier for us."

"So, to answer your question, no. The idea of another intelligent species showing up does not fill me with a sense of ease," Maki said.

I was speechless.

Axtin blinked, struggling to find the right words.

"Point taken," Tyehn shrugged when no one else spoke.

"Do you see why I'm alien cautious?" Alessa asked me. "Not anti-alien."

"I suppose," I said slowly. "But I believe General Rouhr's company has gone above and beyond in proving our trustworthy-ness. Or do you disagree?"

Alessa went quiet. I braced myself for a scathing comment about how she would never associate with aliens again after this.

"Yes," she said. "I suppose you have."

She looked at me from the corner of her eye and smile.

Surprised, I smiled back.

"Want to give the map another try?" I suggested after a beat of silence.

"Might as well. We're going in circles as is."

"We're so lost we don't even know if we're going in circles or not," Axtin muttered.

"Don't say that too loudly," Maki insisted. "The survivors are trusting us."

"They deserve to be aware of the situation," Axtin replied.

"Not when they're teetering on the brink of shock," Maki said. "Do you want to be responsible for carrying them out if they go catatonic?"

"Oh, for fuck's sake," my favorite scientist grumbled. "We're not deaf and we're not invalids. Don't treat us as such."

"Just trying to minimize the trauma." Make gave an apologetic wave.

"The only thing that will traumatize me is missing the deadline to submit my dissertation," the scientist snapped.

None of us knew what to say.

"Damn," Alessa nodded. "That's dedication."

"All the more reason to get him and the others out of here," I said.

"Right." Alessa pulled up her wrist unit and pulled up the map. For a moment, I saw a tangle of lines. Satellite scans of the corridors. I didn't want to say it out loud, but it looked hopeless. Luck and educated guesses, indeed.

"Got a better idea of where to go?" Alessa asked.

"Not at all. You?"

"Negative."

"It was worth a try."

"If I had my tools with me, I could fix it," Alessa muttered. "I didn't bring them because I didn't think I'd need them for an excavation assignment."

"If this is an old hospital or asylum, maybe we can find replacements for your tools," I suggested. "There was medical equipment here. There must've been a maintenance area."

"With luck, we'll pass something like a screwdriver as we wander aimlessly through the void."

I started to laugh, but a noise cut me off. A deep growl, not a laugh, reverberated through the corridors.

"Was that the Gorgo?" Maki asked, her voice quivering just above a whisper.

"I don't think so," Tyehn said, stepping in front of her.

"That sounded like some kind of animal," Axtin said.

"Perhaps we aren't the first life forms to discover this place after all," Alessa said.

"Funnily enough, that's not a comforting thought," Maki laughed dryly.

"Hush," I whispered. "Something's moving up ahead."

I expected to see the form of the infested survivor. Instead, a hulking shape lumbered through the darkness. In addition to the growling, there was another sound. It sounded familiar. Almost like....

"Does that sound like a Xathi to you?" Axtin muttered.

A chittering sound snuck in beneath the perpetual growling. It sounded exactly like a Xathi to me.

"Impossible," Maki gasped.

I turned on my flashlight and shone it into the darkness. What stood before me wasn't a Xathi. Not exactly.

It had a crystalized chomping mandible and insect-like legs, but the rest of its body was covered in thick, dark fur.

"That looks like a mutated Bandiduke," Alessa said under her breath.

"The Xathi might've experimented on other species when they spread their hybridism," Tyehn said. "It wouldn't be the first time we've seen something like this."

"Tyehn, Maki, and Alessa," I said. "Get the survivors out of here."

"What are you going to do?" Alessa asked.

"Axtin and I are going to deal with this," I said.

"Maybe it's friendly," Axtin joked.

I slowly reached for the weapon strapped to my side. The moment my fingertips grazed the hilt, the

Xathi creature went ballistic. It was like it knew what I was doing.

"Get the survivors out," I shouted.

The creature charged through the corridor. Axtin and I nodded to each other and charged.

ALESSA

I was vaguely aware of movement happening around me. Maki and Tyehn ran past me in the direction of the survivors.

I should've helped them but I couldn't make myself move. My feet turned to lead. I couldn't hear anything over the pounding of my own heart.

A blur of movement caught my attention.

Navat charged the terrible creature, weapon brandished.

My first instinct was to cry out to him, to call him away from the danger. I couldn't make my mouth work. It was like my tongue had twisted itself into knots and lodged itself within my throat. I couldn't speak. I couldn't make even the tiniest nose.

My gaze zeroed in on the terrible creature at the

end of the corridor. Its long snout overflowing with thick, jagged teeth snapped at Navat. Nausea rose in my throat as the sight of the beast threw me back to a terrible childhood memory.

I was a little girl, no more than six. I was walking in the jungle with my brothers and sisters. I was the youngest, so it was difficult for me to keep up.

I was running through the part of the jungle that crept up to the back of our house. We weren't allowed to go in at all. One of the first lessons we learned as children was that the forest was unsafe.

My oldest brother, Garreth, was nearly fifteen at the time. He'd decided that the rules of our childhood no longer applied to him, being a grown man and all. He marched into the forest bravely, just to prove that he could. Naturally, the rest of us followed.

I didn't realize everyone had gone into the jungle. If I hadn't seen my older sister's dark braid flick as she disappeared into the tree line, I never would've realized. Not wanting to be the only one left out, and subject myself to ridicule for not tagging alone, I chased after them.

I ran as fast as I could over the bumpy roots and slippery undergrowth. I was so out of breath that I couldn't muster the strength to call out for my siblings. At the time, becoming hopelessly lost hadn't occurred to me.

I still didn't know which one of my siblings screamed first, but it was a sound I'd never forget.

I wasn't sure if my siblings disturbed the Bandiduke or if it happened to stumble upon them. Either way, I found them right as the Bandiduke rose up on its hind legs to take a swipe at Garreth. Its claws nearly took his arm off.

I still remembered the way Garreth's blood dripped onto the carpet of dead leaves. Some got on my shoes.

I don't remember how we got Garreth out of the jungle. I was useless then. I was so terrified that I couldn't move, just like I was now. Except this time, I didn't have my siblings to snap me out of it. My older sister carried me out of the jungle that day. Anyone would think I was the one that nearly lost my arm from the way I screamed and cried.

Garreth survived. He recovered full use of his arm. He was traipsing around in the jungle again within a year. I never left my parents yard again, no matter how much they ridiculed me.

Every once in a while, I dreamt about that day in the jungle. I'd wake up in a cold sweat, shaking and on the verge of tears. No matter what I did, I couldn't let it go. That day haunted me. It would do so for the rest of my life.

The Bandiduke-Xathi monstrosity looked at me. I felt it's gaze, a hunter's gaze, penetrate me down to the core. I trembled under the weight of its stare. I was easy prey.

"Alessa!" Navat's voice drew my attention away from the monster. He stood in front of me, large hands gripped my shoulders. "You need to get to cover, right now!"

Somehow, the meaning of his words worked through my paralyzing fear and clicked into place.

"Be careful," I blurted as I backed away from him. I turned at the last minute, hurtling down the path I believed Maki, Tyehn and the rest of the survivors to have taken.

My heart nearly exploded when something reached out for me in the darkness.

I swung blindly. My hand came into clumsy contact with something solid.

"Alessa." It was Maki's voice. "We're right here."

As my eyes adjusted to the low light, I saw that she'd found a small room. It might've been a closet when this place was functional.

"Sorry," I rasped. "Did I strike you?"

"You grazed me," she said dismissively.

She led me into the room just as Axtin and Navat darted by the opening. The twisted Bandiduke lumbered after them. I held my breath and gripped Maki's hand with all of my might. She gripped me back. I felt her trembling beside me. It almost made me feel better to know I wasn't the only one terrified out of my mind.

I clamped a hand over my mouth to contain the scream that threatened to spill out. The twisted Bandiduke stopped at the opening and sniffed. It smelled us, I was certain of that.

Possibly means of escape flew through my head, all of them ended in death between the jaws of that terrible beast.

Something came down on its head. It looked like the head of a large hammer. The Bandiduke tore its focus from the opening and lumbered after whatever struck it. I assumed it was Axtin.

"Let's move farther back," Tyehn whispered. "There's another chamber."

Slowly, taking great care to not make any noise, I got to my feet. Maki and I clung to each other as we ushered the survivors deeper into the darkness. Tyehn led the way, illuminating his headlamp every few feet to make sure we weren't going to wall ourselves in by mistake.

We settled farther away from where the battle against the Bandiduke raged. Putting distance between myself and the creature should've made me feel better but it didn't. Just knowing that thing was somewhere inside this structure with us was enough to keep me on a knives edge.

All I could see in my mind's eye was the bloody, gushing wound on Garreth's arm that fateful day. The thought of Navat bearing similar injuries made me feel sick to my stomach. I still heard the sounds of fighting. I figured that was a good sign. I'd worry when things went too quiet.

Another noise caught my attention. This wasn't part of the fight. It sounded far closer than that. A low, keening sound came from within the chamber.

"Tyehn," I whisper-shouted. "Turn on your light."

He did as I asked.

"What's that sound?" I asked.

"It's him!" One of the survivors shouted.

Tyehn turned the beam of his light onto a man who'd pushed himself into the corner.

It was the scientist we'd worked with above.

The one who appeared to dislike Navat for no reason at all.

"Are you all right?" I called to him. I felt like an asshole for still not knowing his name.

I didn't want him to know that, though.

Not right now. I'd ask him later, once we figured out what was wrong with him.

"He doesn't look right," Tyehn said.

"You don't think it's…" Maki trailed off. She didn't need to finish her sentence. I knew what she was thinking.

Had the scientist fallen victim to a Gorgo?

The scientist craned his neck around at an unnatural angle. I swore I heard bones crack and pop. His eyes didn't look right.

"I'm so sorry," I whispered. I don't know why it occurred to me to say that. It's not like he could understand me now.

"Everyone, get back," Tyehn urged.

The survivors scrambled to get away from the scientist, who lashed out at them with frenzied sweeps.

"Got a stun gun?" I asked Maki.

"An empty one," she replied.

"Shit."

The scientist let out a harrowing screech and launched himself at us. Without thinking about it, I kicked out, the heel of my hiking boot slamming into his ribs.

He stumbled back. The Gorgo inside him genuinely didn't expect me to fight back.

That Gorgo was in for a rude awakening.

My grip on my temper was fraying, and at the moment I was having a hard time coming up with reasons to stay calm.

"What do we have for weapons?" I demanded.

"We can't risk using a gun or a blaster in here," Tyehn replied as he yanked the Gorgo infested scientist away from Maki and me. "The chamber is too small. It could ricochet and hit one of the others."

"What are our options?" I asked, wrenching my hand back in order to launch my fist into the scientist's face. He screeched in pain.

I had to remember that it wasn't him anymore. Annoying as he'd been, he was lost to the Gorgo.

"I have a knife," Tyehn said.

"That'll do. Hand it over," I requested.

"What?"

"Hand. It. Over," I said through gritted teeth as the infected scientist broke free and started rabidly clawing at Tyehn's arm. "Think about it. The optics of you fighting a human are much worse than me doing it. Plus I have a score I want to settle after having gone through all this."

"I have a better idea." He shoved the scientist off of him and drew the knife from his belt. When he came at him again, he lifted the knife.

At the last second, he realigned himself and went right for the hand clutching the knife.

The shock caused Tyehn to drop it. It clattered to the floor. I darted in and scooped it up before the scientist could.

"Tyehn's been bitten," I said to Maki. "Does that mean he's going to be infested by a Gorgo, too?"

"I don't think so. They're not werewolves." Maki said. "But that doesn't mean a bite is a good thing."

Tyehn kicked the scientist in the stomach. Realizing he couldn't out muscle the Valorni, the possessed turned to me.

"Bring it, bitch," I hissed. He lunged at me as I sliced the knife through the air, taking a piece of him with me. He reeled back with a howl and thick, dark red blood oozed from the fresh wound.

He gaped at me and for a moment looked as if he was going to attempt another attack.

The rational part of the Gorgo inhabiting his body must've decided otherwise.

He took off running.

Navat and Axtin must've still been fighting the horrible Bandiduke. The last thing they should have to deal with is a rabid scientist causing a distraction.

I took a deep breath, clutched the hilt of Tyehn's knife, and sprinted after him.

Tyehn needed to stay with the survivors and protect them.

Years of training, years of learning to work with my temper, were all for this.

I was best placed to do this.

And I would succeed.

NAVAT

I fired the last round of ammunition in my weapon. Just as it had the last fifty times I fired, the ammo bounced off the Xathi half breed monstrosity as if they were made of foam.

"What the hell is this thing?" Axtin grunted as dodged a sideswipe from its crystalized talons.

"How has it survived all this time?" I shot back. "We've been running planet-wide scans for Xathi every day since the invasion. How did we not know about this?"

"Let's save the debrief for when this thing is actually dead, okay?" Axtin smashed his hammer into the creature's skull. I didn't hear the crunch I expected to hear, but the blow dazed the animal.

"Looks like we're going to have to do this the old-fashioned way, huh?" I sighed.

"I don't do it any other way," Axtin grinned before launching himself at the creature again.

I pulled a small staff from my belt. It was only a few inches in length until I pressed the little silver button on the side.

The staff extended into a two-foot pole with two large, spiked spheres on either end. I briefly wondered if it would be strong enough against the crystallized exoskeleton of the hybrid creature.

I had the mace made from a special Urai metal alloy but I'd yet to test it. I supposed now was as good a time as any.

I charged forward.

The creature was busy trying to dodge Axtin's furious hammer swings. It didn't see me come around it's left flank.

I let the mace fly. I wasn't sure who was more surprised, me or the creature. The spikes of the mace dug into it's crystalized hide.

With a sharp yank, shards clattered to the ground. Beneath the crystal growths was a normal, fleshly body.

"Chip away at the growths," I called to Axtin.

Axtin swung his hammer at a jagged growth on what I assumed was the creature's shoulder. It took a few tries but it eventually crumbled away.

The creature realized what we were doing and doubled down on its aggressive attacks. It snarled and snapped. It swiped and clawed.

I moved a fraction of a second too late and took a talon to the arm. Warm, wet blood gushed down my bicep. I'd deal with that later.

I caught a glimpse of Axtin. He'd taken a few blows as well. The side of his face was caked with blood, though I couldn't tell if it was his or the creature's.

He let his hammer fly, striking the creature in the side of the face. This time, I heard the crunch I wanted to hear.

It fell over on its side, dazed and struggling.

"Go for the belly," Axtin shouted.

The creatures soft underside was exposed. I swung my mace and kept swinging until its blood covered my arms and its howls fell silent.

"Is it dead?" I rasped.

"It's pulp," Axtin snorted.

I looked down at the creature's body. Its entire midsection was completely unrecognizable. Chunks of flesh and intestines littered the floor.

"Think there's any chance of reanimation?" I asked.

"That would require a nearby Xathi. I think we're safe on that end."

"If this creature managed to survive all these

months, there are probably more roaming around just like it."

"We'll deal with that once we get out of here," Axtin shook his head.

"Our work is never done."

"That's what we get for ruining someone else's planet," I sighed.

"We didn't ruin it. The Xathi did. Are you telling me you're not happy we're here?"

"It's not that," I said. "This planet is fine. I enjoy helping the humans get back on their feet after all the destruction."

"But?" Axtin prompted.

"It isn't any different to me than any of the other places I've lived," I shrugged.

"Really?" Axtin blinked in surprise. "I hated this place at first. I mean, I really hated it. Now, I can't imagine living anywhere else."

"That's because your mate lives here," I smirked.

"Yours probably does too." Axtin nudged my shoulder. "You and Alessa seem to get along."

"Are you kidding?" I scoffed. "We've been at each other's throats since we met."

Except for when we weren't. Except for when her body had pressed against mine, the taste of her sweet lips on my tongue.

"That's how Leena and I were," he said. "We hated each other at first."

"Nothing is going to happen between Alessa and me," I insisted. "Especially not if we die down here."

"Whatever you say," Axtin said with a knowing smirk. "Where do you think the others went?"

"I'm not sure. We covered a lot of ground in that fight. I couldn't tell you where we're standing let alone where they could be."

"Time to pick a direction and start walking?"

"Yup."

We walked away from the creature, heading back the way we believed we'd come.

"Is that one of the tombs?" Axtin pointed at an archway.

"No, I think that's an empty room."

"This is ridiculous. We're never going to find them again."

"With luck, we'll find a way out instead."

Axtin gave me a look.

"You'd really leave them behind?"

"Of course not!" I snapped. "If we find a way out we can call for help. We can get another excavation team in here or use a heat sensor. Something. Anything. We'd be more useless up there than we are down here."

"Wait," Axtin cut me off. "Do you hear that?"

I listened closely. A low, keening noise permeated the silence.

"Maki?" I called. "Tyehn?"

The keening became a shriek.

"Srell, that sounds like a Gorgo possession," Axtin groaned.

"Come on." I jogged ahead.

"Why do you want to go towards it?" Axtin jogged after me.

"It doesn't sound like the one from before. It could be one of the survivors."

"They aren't survivors anymore," Axtin muttered.

I cast a dark look over my shoulder.

"Too blunt?"

"What do you think?"

"Sorry, I just spent an hour hacking apart a Xathi beast. Forgive me if I'm a little crass."

A scream cut off my reply, quickly followed by the sound of bare feet smacking against the floor.

A figure rounded the corner. I recognized my special scientist adversary immediately.

"Oh, no," I sighed.

"Help!" He screeched, clawing at his face and arms.

Suddenly, his face shifted. A nasty snarl took over his expression.

"There's no help for you now. Give in!"

It was the voice of the Gorgo.

His looked at me, his eyes wild and shining in the dark.

I held still, waiting to see what he'd do. I gripped my mace loosely, ready to swing in case he attacked.

"She's coming," he rasped before rushing forward. I expected him to lunge for me but he ran around me instead.

"Who's coming?" Axtin blinked in confusion.

Another set of footfalls echoed through the dark corridor. Alessa appeared out of the murk, covered in blood and dirty, wielding a knife as big as her arm.

"Don't trust him," Alessa warned us. "He just tried to kill us."

"Hosts! Hosts! Hosts!" The scientist shrieked, tipping his head back farther than it should've been able to go. "We need hosts!"

"I don't have a choice, do I?" I looked at Axtin.

"You know it has to be done," he shrugged.

"No!" The scientist wailed. "I will have a host!"

He lunged at me.

I swung my mace.

His neck made a sickening crack before he fell to the ground.

"What the fuck?" Alessa demanded.

"I'm sorry," I put my mace away and turned to face her. "I'm sorry you had to see that."

Except... she didn't seem particularly traumatized.

If anything, she was mad.

At me.

"I've just chased that thing through who know's how many miles of tunnels, and you just bop it, and it's dead?" She stopped over to the body and glared at it."

"I didn't realize it was so important to you." I struggled over my word. This was not the reaction I was expecting.

"Those things destroyed my team, ruined my dig site, and tried to kill me. I've earned the right to take a little revenge."

"You're right," I agreed because I didn't know what else to do. "Are you all right otherwise?"

"I'm fine," she muttered. "The others might not be. Let's go."

Without another word, she tucked the knife into her belt loop and jogged off into the darkness.

"She's the perfect mate for you," Axtin teased before rushing after her. "Grumpy, a little homicidal, unpredictable..."

Perfect.

Couldn't be. She was fascinating, sure. Smart, beautiful, could hold her own.

But not my mate.

But I jogged after her anyway.

ALESSA

I didn't check to see if Axtin and Navat followed me.
I assumed they did.

If they weren't smart enough to follow me without being told to do so, I didn't have much faith in them to ensure my survival.

I slowed my pace to take a breath.

I knew I wasn't being fair to Axtin or Navat. They'd just risked their lives to kill that terrible…thing. I was just frazzled.

Frazzled was an understatement. I was teetering on the verge of a meltdown but I refused to let myself fall. I had to keep it together.

I simply wasn't expecting to confront a childhood fear, be attacked by a colleague, and be at risk from a Gorgo possession within the span of ten minutes.

I believed I deserved a moment to have a little temper tantrum. It would've been therapeutically beneficial for me to kill the scientist.

Maybe.

Secretly, I felt glad Navat did it. Even with the anger and fear coursing through my veins, intensifying everything, I don't think I could've done it.

He still looked normal for the most part. Even though he had a Gorgo crawling around in his brain.

The thought of it made me feel sick. I stumbled and braced myself against the wall.

"Alessa," came Navat's voice. I felt his hand on my shoulder. Two conflicting instincts raged inside me. Part of me wanted to pull away. The other part of me wanted to sink closer to him. I didn't understand it. I didn't understand anything right now.

"I..." I tried to speak but my voice cracked.

"It's okay if you need to take a minute," he said with surprising gentleness.

"What a lovely picture," Axtin said.

"Shut up," Navat grumbled. The pang of brotherly annoyance in his voice made me smile. I'd used that tone with my brothers more times than I could count.

"I'm fine," I said once I was able to find my voice again. "Just felt a little sick. That's not a sign of a Gorgo testing me out as a host, is it?"

"Not that we've observed," Navat said.

"I'm sure you meant that to be comforting," I forced a smile. I still felt nauseous and terribly panicked, but it was manageable now.

A scream tore my attention away from Navat.

"Shit," I whispered.

"What was that?"

"We have to move," I pleaded. "I think another survivor has been possessed."

"Shit," Axtin and Navat echoed. We sprinted through the dimly lit corridors. I clipped my shoulder on an archway that was narrower than I anticipated but pushed on.

I led them to the room where we'd hidden earlier. I was shocked to see a dead body on the floor. For a moment, that's all I was able to look at.

"Alessa, look out!" Navat yanked me back a step just as another Gorgo possesed human launched at me.

"How many are there?" I cried.

"Too many," Maki called back to me. She had one on it's back, her knee between its shoulder blades. "The possession came through so quickly. We couldn't do anything to prevent it."

As far as I knew, there wasn't anything anyone could do to prevent it but I didn't want to say as much right now.

Another one of the possessed launched at Maki,

grabbing her around the neck in an attempt to haul her off its companion.

She tried to scream, but the damn thing had closed off her airway.

I ran at it before I could think twice. My hands wrapped around its neck and I began to squeeze. It clawed at my hands, leaving rake marks on my skin. Its distraction gave Maki a chance to dispatch the one beneath her, wheel around and fire a shot into the skull of the one on top of her.

"Good teamwork," she barked out a humorless laugh.

Our reprieve didn't last long. Another one of the possessed came at me. This time, I drew the knife I'd lifted off Tyehn.

I was ready and waiting, then the possessed one slammed into me. I drove the knife between its ribs again and again until it went still.

Another one of the possessed hovered in the corner of the room, its eyes gleaming with madness. It looked as if it were considering attacking. I bared my teeth and lunged at it. Instead of meeting me for a fight, it scurried away into the darkness. Anything human about it was long gone. It had been less than an hour since the scientist's mind was taken.

"How many are left?" I dreaded the question but I had to ask it.

"Just us," A small voice said. Two survivors from the team of scientists remained. None of my crew. One male. One female. The female had been the one to speak.

"What's your name?" I asked her. I should've asked long ago. I should've known all their names.

"Bayla," she replied.

"I'm Kip," the man said.

"Good to meet you," I said and then laughed at the awkwardness of my words.

"Odd time to exchange pleasantries, isn't it?" Navat said. He put his mace away, a bloodied body as his feet.

He looked at the shredded body beside me.

"Did you do that?"

"I did."

"Just with a knife?" He pointed to the knife still buried in the body .

"I was scared for my life," I replied.

"Nice work," he nodded in approval.

"Thanks. I never want to do that again," I said.

"I thought you liked claiming your kills," he asked, one eyebrow raised and a small smirk on his lips.

"I like stopping those who want to hurt me," I replied.

"Fair enough."

"Tyehn might want this back," I said as I ripped the knife out of the limp body. I thanked the stars for adrenaline. I'd never be able to do get through this without losing my mind without it. I dreaded the moment it wore off.

"Speaking of Tyehn, where did he go?"

"Wasn't he just here?" Maki asked, her voice pinched with fear.

"I thought so." Another wave of panic rose up inside me.

A harsh scuttling sound rang out.

"Skrell!" Tyehn's voice was unmistakable.

"Where the hell is he?" Maki demanded. She took off, following his voice and the sounds that came with it.

We found him a few chambers over, locked in battle with the most terrifying creature I'd ever seen.

"What fresh hell is this?" I cried.

The creature had a heavily armored body surrounded by at least ten thorny legs. It was twice the size of Tyehn, who darted between its legs as he sliced.

"Oh my god," Maki smacked her hand over her mouth. Tears welled in her eyes.

"Get back," Navat instructed.

He didn't need to tell me twice. After killing the possessed ones, I had no desire to get tangled up with whatever the fuck that was.

"How many nightmarish creatures are hidden in

here?" I whispered as I pulled Maki back. I'd never seen her look so scared.

"I just want Tyehn to be safe," Maki whimpered. "I've never had to worry about someone besides myself before."

"He'll be fine," I assured her. "They're tough. More than tough."

I couldn't let her break down on us now. We needed her.

I risked a glance at the men battling the monster. It wasn't going well. It had too many legs. It blocked their every move.

From what I could tell, it looked like it was protecting its underside. That was the weak spot for most creatures on this planet, aside from our sentient trees. This creature appeared to be doing everything it could to stop Tyehn, Navat, and Axtin from getting underneath it.

That gave me an idea.

I still had Tyehn's knife.

"Whatever you do," I told Maki, "don't move."

"What are you going to do?"

"Something stupid," I replied.

I waited until the creature's back, or what I assumed was it's back, was turned to me before darting forward. It was preoccupied with Tyehn's guns, Axtin's hammer, and Navat's mace. It didn't see me slip between its two backmost legs.

Something pinched my left side, but I brushed it off.

I drew the blade and shoved it between two of the armored plates. The monster shrieked and thrashed about, trying to reach me.

Tyehn fired a few shots and the monster went rigid. I scrambled away from it just as it collapsed, dead.

"Fuck," I sighed. "What the hell was that thing? I've never seen anything like it before."

Maki, Tyehn, Axtin, and Navat just stared at me. They were all giving me strange looks.

"What?" I demanded. I tried to take a step forward but pain shot through my left side. My legs buckled. "What's happening?"

Navat and Maki knelt beside me.

"Don't worry," Maki soothed. "You're going to be okay."

"Okay?" I repeated. "What are you talking about?"

It was then that I saw it. Protruding from my side was one of the thorns from that monster's leg. How had I not noticed it?

The damn adrenaline.

"What should I do?" I asked. "Do I pull it out?"

"No," Navat said quickly. "Whatever you do, don't touch it. It's stopping you from bleeding out."

"But it hurts," I whimpered. The pain was

unbearable now. "Please, help me. I don't want to die down here."

"I know," Navat said. "You won't. We're going to figure something out, right?" He looked to the others, who nodded nervously.

They didn't believe I was going to be okay. I could see it in their eyes.

"Just rest," Navat urged. "Rest while we think."

"Okay," I nodded.

Within moments, everything went black. I didn't want to go into the darkness, but I couldn't make it stop.

NAVAT

This was bad. This was really bad.

That thorn was deep in Alessa's side. If I removed it, she would bleed out in minutes. I couldn't very well leave it in, either. We had to do something before she went into shock. I wasn't about to lose another member of this team. Not her. Not after all she'd survived.

"What do we do?" Maki asked.

"Med packs," I blurted. "Who has one."

"I have part of one," Axtin offered. "That Xathi-hybrid creature damaged the package."

Axtin showed me a torn up med back strapped to his hip.

"Do you think the stuff that fell out is still in the tunnels?" I asked.

"It's possible. I'll check it out."

"Take Tyehn with you," I ordered.

Tyehn followed Axtin without argument.

"What do you want me to do?" Maki asked.

"Get her into a better position, if you can."

I looked back at Alessa and saw that her eyes were closed.

"Oh, no." I leaned in close to her, listening for breath. It was there, but it was far too faint. She didn't have long.

"What do we need?" Maki asked, slowly shifting Alessa's body so that she was flat on her back. Maki placed Alessa's head in her lap. I could almost pretend Alessa was sleeping.

"Something to close the wound," I said. "There's a spray in the med packs that's good for patching up wounds."

"Is she going to need stitches?"

"I'd prefer not to use those," I said. "They can split open. We're going to need her to be mobile once we get her back on her feet."

"She's so pale," Maki observed. "What if that thing had poisoned thorns?"

I hadn't considered that. It was a very real possibility.

"Stay with her. I'll check it out."

I walked over to the spindly carcass of the hellish

creature. I used my flashlight to examine the thorns on its legs. They didn't smell toxic and they didn't appear to be covered in any kind of substance.

"I don't see anything that indicates poison," I said. "Let's hope that's the case. The med packs usually only have a general antidote."

"It probably won't work if she has been poisoned," Maki said. "I've never seen anything like that before. Not even in the wilderness guides."

"Let's hope it's the only one."

"I found some stuff," Axtin trotted back into the room with Tyehn on his heels.

"Let me see," I ordered.

Axtin held out his hands. Bandages, antibiotic pills, some kind of antifungal ointment and – ah-ha!

"Perfect," I sighed with relief and grabbed the small canister of cell repair spray from his hands.

"We're going to have to remove the thorn now," I said. "Maki, I'll need you to spray the wound."

"Me?" She stammered. "Can't you do it?"

"Sure, if you want to pull the thorn out of her."

"Never mind. I'll spray," she said.

"I thought you might say that. Do we have anything for pain?" I asked.

"Don't think so," Tyehn shook his head. "That spray should have a numbing agent inside it."

"Let's hope it's strong enough."

I took a small utility knife from my belt and used it to cut around the fabric of Alessa's shirt. A ring of skin was exposed around the thorn.

"I hope you have good aim," I said to Maki.

"Just shut up and do it. You're making me nervous," she snapped.

I carefully took the top of the thorn between pinched fingers. It was at least two inches thick around and a good six inches long. Four inches stuck out of Alessa's side.

"I'm sorry if this hurts," I whispered to her.

I gripped the thorn and pulled slowly at first. It didn't budge. I wondered if it was covered in barbs. It might cause even more damage coming out than it did going in.

I pulled harder. Blood spurted from her side. The thorn had to come out right now before she bled to death but it was like it was fighting me.

"Skrell," I swore and yanked as hard as I could. The thorn flew out of her side.

Maki dove in and coated the gushing wound with the cell regrowth spray until the small canister was empty.

I grabbed the bandages and pressed them against her wound. They quickly soaked through with blood but I kept the pressure on. The cell regrowth spray didn't take long to work. She just had to hold on until then.

"She's going to be short a few liters of blood," Tyehn observed. "We probably shouldn't move her too soon."

"I don't know if we'll have that option," Axtin said. "Some of those Gorgos ran off. They'll probably be back."

"Are they attracted to the smell of blood?" Maki asked.

"Not that we know of."

"What, exactly, do we know?" She demanded.

"Not much," Axtin replied. "Just that they only seem interested in humans and human bodies aren't strong enough to contain them for long."

"Comforting," Maki smirked. "But I already knew that."

"Then why'd you ask?"

"Because I was seriously hoping for some good news, okay?" She replied. "It's easier to fight these things if I know more about them."

"The lab is working on it. Hopefully, they've gotten some more test subjects," Tyehn said.

I listened to their back and forth while I kept my eyes on Alessa. I watched her chest to make sure she was still breathing. I watched her wound to see if the cell regrowth spray worked.

The bleeding had slowed, but it hadn't come to a

complete stop yet. I pressed the pads of my fingers against her wrist. Her pulse was just barely there.

"I don't suppose anyone has any spare blood on them?" I asked.

"I left my blood bags at home," Maki joked.

"If any of that spray happened to get inside her wound, it'll help generate new blood cells," Tyehn said.

"It definitely got in her wound," Maki said. "I'd say more of it got inside than outside."

"Then she has a fighting chance," I said. "So long as she doesn't bleed out all of the new blood cells."

"How optimistic of you," Axtin said.

"I'm a realist."

Alessa suddenly let out a sigh. Her eyelids fluttered, but wouldn't open.

"Take it easy," I whispered to her. "You've been injured. You're probably in a lot of pain, but I need you to keep still."

"It hurts." Her voice was nothing more than a faint wheeze.

"I know," I said. "But it'll pass. You've already made it through the worst part."

Or so I hoped. Relief flooded over me with such force that it knocked the breath out of my chest.

"What happened?" She asked.

"You kicked ass, that's what happened," Axtin laughed. "But right now, we need to talk and walk."

"You saved our lives," I told her as I gently lifted her in my arms, heart thumping so loud it almost drowned out the sound of my own voice. "You're damn good with a blade."

"Brother taught me." She spoke in halting breaths. I almost didn't want her to speak, but I figured it was a good way to distract her from the pain as her body healed.

"You have a brother? Older or younger?" I asked.

"Two. Both older."

"What about sisters?"

"Two. Both older," she repeated.

"Oh, so you're the youngest," I said. "I'm the oldest of my siblings but we never spent much time together."

I didn't know why I was telling her this. I supposed I hoped it would help her.

"Why not?"

She opened her eyes. Her vision looked unfocused but the fact that she was looking around was a good sign.

"I had to go earn a living," I explained. "I didn't have much growing up so as soon as I was able, I left. I couldn't be an unnecessary financial burden on my parents."

"That sounds rough."

"It wasn't so bad," I shrugged. "I got to live on a lot of different planets, which was always interesting."

"Like what?"

"I lived and worked on a planet that was completely covered in water," I said. "We lived on floating rafts and would put on special suits to do the work we needed to do below the surface."

"I couldn't do that. I'm not a big fan of water. The water here is even more dangerous than the jungles." Alessa looked more alert now. Color returned to her cheeks. I wasn't ready to let her get up and walk around yet.

"The water on that planet wasn't very safe either. Most of the things in it were toxic or venomous. The native populations built up immunity to most things but I wasn't a native so I just had to be extra careful," I explained.

"You're oddly talkative," Alessa observed.

"So are you," I replied. "I never thought you'd tell me about your family."

"You wanted to know about my family?" She furrowed her brow.

"I wanted to know about you," I said. "A knife-wielding, monster-slaying, mechanical engineer like you must have an interesting story."

"Are you just saying that to take my mind off the excruciating pain in my side?"

"Yes, but I genuinely am curious," I said.

"Prove it."

I wasn't expecting that response.

"Um," I stammered. "Did you always want to be an engineer?"

"I like knowing how things work," she explained. "I've always been good at putting two pieces of nothing together and turning them into a functional something."

"How does that fit into excavations?"

"It's sort of like reverse engineering, I think," she said. "I can see the remains of a functional something, as well as the pieces of nothing they're made from. From there, I can make guesses about the purpose of the functional something. Does that make sense?"

"Yes," I chuckled.

"It also helps to have someone on the team who's good at guessing structural integrity," she said.

"That's a good point. The knife-wielding thing is a big bonus."

"I'm glad to be of use."

She was joking. She'd be fine.

But it'd be a lifetime before I forgot the smell of her blood.

ALESSA

"Do you think you're ready to try walking soon?" Navat asked. "I hate to say it, but I might need my hands in a hurry, and I'd rather not just drop you."

My entire left side still hurt like a bitch but it now felt like severe bruising rather than a gushing puncture wound. I figured it was as good a time as any.

Besides, it had been disturbingly nice to lay in his arms. His warm, spicy smell was comforting.

"Catch me if I fall?" I asked.

"Of course."

His smile made my heart clench. I'd gone to great lengths to keep him at arms-length since I'd been weak, kissed him behind the tents, but now that was harder to do.

He was nice. He was handsome.

He was still kind of an asshole but in a way that made me smile. Plus, he saved my life. That earned some bonus points in my book.

"Move carefully," he advised. "Don't push yourself if it hurts too much."

"Define too much," I asked.

"Eight on a scale of one to ten," he suggested.

"I'm at a solid seven," I replied. "I'll give it a go."

He offered his hand, which I grasped.

"Don't look so nervous," I joked when I saw his worried expression.

"I just want all of us to get out of here alive," he replied.

"Me too."

I counted down from three and he slowly lowered me to my feet. I was unsteady as a newborn Luurizi.

I stumbled forward. He caught me, letting me brace myself against him.

"Easy," he said softly.

"I'm okay," I assured him. "Just a little lightheaded."

"You lost a considerable amount of blood," he said.

"It's true. It's all right back there." Axtin pointed down the tunnel behind us.

Navat caught my chin in his hand before I could look.

"Probably best if you don't look at it."

"You're probably right," I agreed. I looked to Maki instead. "Any ideas on what to do?"

"Besides making sure you don't keel over?" She jested. "Not really. We're back where we started, in a sense."

"What about those bodies we found?" Bayla asked.

I'd completely forgotten about those strange burial rooms we'd stumbled across.

"What about them?" Axtin asked.

Bayla looked at him from the corner of her eye. It was obvious that she was terrified of him. I wondered if she was terrified of all the aliens.

I couldn't blame her. She'd seen them do some fairly terrifying things even if those things were done to ensure her safety.

"It's just that those burials seem to be the only real clue as to what this place is," she said. "Maybe if we figure out what they're for, we can figure out how to leave."

"It's as reasonable as anything we've done so far," Maki shrugged. "Besides, those burials were really cool. I'd love to take another look at them."

"I can't think of a better idea," Tyehn agreed. "Let's do it."

"Can you make it that far?" Navat asked me.

"I'll have to go slowly," I said.

"You five go on ahead," Navat urged the others. "Alessa and I will catch up."

"No way," Axtin shook his head. "If you two are left alone, you're practically defenseless."

"He's right," I said. "If one of the surviving infected ones shows up, neither of us will be able to fight."

"I will if I drop you," he smirked.

"Drop me and I'll slice your ankles," I threatened playfully.

"I'll be your escort," Axtin declared. "Maki and Tyehn can look out for the other two."

"Works for us," Kip replied. "Got any weapons to spare?"

"Sorry," Tyehn chuckled. "I can't give you a weapon unless you show me proof of training. They aren't made for humans."

"Can't blame me for asking," Kip said.

Maki, Tyehn, Kip, and Bayla quickly left the chamber. Axtin stayed behind and kept a watchful eye on me and Navat as he helped me walk.

"Does it hurt?" Navat asked.

"I had a thorn as long as my arm in my side. Of course, it hurts. I'll live."

"Apologies for crashing your alone time," Axtin said with a knowing smirk.

"Shut up," Navat and I said at the same time.

"It appears I've struck a nerve." Axtin walked out of the chamber ahead of us and peered into the corridor. "It looks clear if you want to get a move on. Do you want me to walk in front or behind?"

"Behind. I feel like these things are more likely to sneak up from behind."

"After you," Axtin swept his arm through the doorway.

Navat and I struggled to walk, at first. My legs were unsteady. Putting too much pressure on my left side hurt like hell. Eventually, we worked out a rhythm and started moving along at a fair pace.

"I should've let Tyehn do this," Axtin grumbled behind us.

"I'm sorry we're not speedy enough for you," I called over my shoulder.

Navat kept one arm wrapped securely around my waist. I felt weightless in his grip though he still allowed me to pull my weight, so to speak.

I appreciated him for that. I hated feeling useless, especially in situations like this where it was vital that everyone contributed to the group's survival. Granted, I'd never been in a situation like this before but I knew I couldn't allow myself to become useless.

"I heard something," Navat whisper. All three of us went still.

Something was definitely moving up ahead.

Axtin shone his flashlight, illuminating a figure. Fear seized in my heart. I was in no condition to fight or flee.

"You scared the wits out of us, Tyehn," Axtin sighed.

"Apologies. That was the opposite of what I was trying to do," he said.

"What is it? Why have you doubled back?" I asked.

"There's something you need to see. It's waiting for us."

"It?" Navat said.

"One of the infected ones," Tyehn explained. "It wants to talk to us."

"What?" I blurted.

"That's what it says. It's standing there calmly. It said it would wait until we're all there. It knows you're hurt. It told me to tell you not to rush," Tyehn explained. He looked aware of how odd his words were.

"How do you know this isn't a trap?" Navat asked.

"I think it would've attacked us by now if it was," Tyehn said. "Besides, why would it want more people in the room with it? It's seen us fight. It knows it can't beat all of us."

"Isn't this what you wanted?" I asked Navat. "I thought your people had a lab where they were studying these things."

"This isn't what I had in mind," Navat said.

"This might be your only chance to have a conversation with one of them," I said.

"Are you sure it's infected?" Axtin asked Tyehn.

"I'm certain of it," Tyehn insisted. "We should talk to it."

"Let's go," I said to Navat. "What's the worst that could happen?"

"You're joking, right? You almost died an hour ago."

"But I didn't," I grinned.

"What if it infects you?" He asked.

"What if it doesn't? What if this is our one chance to get some answers?"

"I'm making an executive decision," Axtin said. "We're going."

He offered an arm to me.

"I'll take over your transportation issue," he jested.

"Fine. We'll go," Navat grumbled and tightened his grip around my waist. "For the record, I think it's a terrible idea."

Axtin resumed his position behind us as Navat and I followed Tyehn. On the way to the burial chambers, we passed the body of that terrible Bandiduke mutant. I looked away until it was behind us. If Navat noticed, he didn't say anything. I was grateful for that. I'd shown enough vulnerability for one day.

Had it only been a day? I couldn't tell. It felt like we'd been down here for ages.

We entered the first burial chamber. Sure enough, one of the infected survivors that had run off stood in the center of the room with a strange smile on its face.

No, not it. Her.

Her red hair was dirty and matted. Her body was covered in scrapes and bruises. She smiled when she saw us.

"Ah, at last."

Her voice didn't sound right. It sounded like twenty voices layered on top of one another.

"What do you want?" Navat snarled.

"You should address us with more respect," she gave him a reproachful look.

Us?

"I don't think so," Navat replied.

"Don't antagonize her," I warned him.

"Listen to the girl," she said. "We should suck out your eyes for trying to kill us."

"We?" Maki asked softly.

"Don't pretend you do not know us," she snapped. "We are ancient and inevitable."

"Are you the Gorgoxians?" Axtin asked.

She smiled. There were too many teeth in her mouth. The sight of her made me feel sick to my stomach. I clung to Navat without realizing it. He tightened his grip around me.

"We are meant to rule all," she continued. "We are all-powerful. We are all-knowing. Allow us to rule over you. Through subjugation, you will find salvation."

"That's not how this works," Axtin chuckled.

"How small you are," she sneered. "Yet, you do not realize it. None of you do. The illusion of free will is fading away. Embrace it or we will make you."

She tipped her head back and let out a shrill laugh. Something underneath her features shifted, but I couldn't make it out.

Suddenly, her limbs started flailing. Her entire body trembled from head to toe.

"What's happening?" I whispered.

"I don't know," Navat whispered back. He drew his mace and held it at the ready.

"Should we help her?" Maki asked.

"What could we do?" Tyehn countered.

"We should kill her," Axtin said.

"No way," Maki protested. "She's valuable whether she wants to murder us or not."

The woman stopped shaking. She crumbled to the ground and went still.

"Is she dead?" I asked after a few moments.

"I'm not sure."

Before any of us could check for a pulse, she lifted her head. She looked at each of us, then stood up as if nothing had happened. She opened her mouth as if to speak.

"Hello."

NAVAT

The voice that came out of the infected human wasn't the same as the voice that the Gorgos used. This new voice was deep and gentle, but it didn't match the appearance of the human, either.

"Who are we speaking to now?" Maki asked, apparently on the same train of thought as me.

"I am called Thijn," the human replied.

"What are you?" Alessa asked softly. She was looking a little pale once more.

"I dare not speak the name of my people," Thijn said. "The others are watching. I wish not to evoke their wrath further."

"What are you doing inside that human?" I demanded.

"I needed a vessel," Thijn explained.

"You mean a host?" Alessa sneered.

"No," Thijn protested. "Not a host. I am not here to claim this body as my own. I only wish to borrow it."

"Borrowing without permission is called stealing," Maki pointed out.

"I had no other choice. I'm not strong enough to take a vessel on my own. This body was already in use. I slipped in when the other being slipped out."

"Don't you have your own body to use?" Axtin asked.

"Indeed." Thijn pointed to one of the burials. "However, mine is incapable of supporting life."

"You're one of them?" Alessa gasped.

"Yes."

"Then you know what this place is," I said.

"I wish I did not," Thijn sighed. Sadness clouded the eyes of the human vessel. "My people lived here long ago. We were a simple people, but prosperous. Like the society that roams this planet now, we had a good relationship with the earth beneath us and the creatures around us."

"What happened?"

"An enemy far older than us came to this planet," Thijn continued. "To this day, I do not know what they wanted with us."

"What did they do?"

"They built this place," Thijn looked around with a

mournful gaze. "We had no idea until it was too late. We did not have settlements here. We were desert dwellers."

"Some of our friends found a temple out in the desert," Axtin said. "Was it yours?"

"I know the place of which you speak but we are not the originators," Thijn explained. "We never disturbed it."

"Why did your enemies build this place?" Maki asked.

"They built it to keep us contained," Thijn's voice dropped to a whisper. "They used to go from settlement to settlement and take whoever they believed worthy. We never understood what qualities they were looking for. They brought us here and experimented on us."

"Were they looking for hosts?" I asked.

"At the time, I did not know. Now that I see what they are doing to your kind," Thijn looked to Alessa, then to Maki. "I believe they were scouting my people for hosts. For what purpose? I do not know."

"Sounds like the Gorgos have done this before," Tyehn sighed.

"Gorgos?" Thijn asked.

"That's what we've been calling them," Axtin explained. "We're trying to get rid of them. Are you sure you don't know anything about them?"

"We figured out how to drive them away," Thijn

said. "But not after taking great losses. Our population never recovered. We died out less than one hundred cycles after they came to this planet."

"But you stopped them?" I asked. "You made them leave?"

"Indeed," Thijn nodded.

"How?" I demanded. "How did your people do it?"

"I cannot say for sure," Thijn said. "My time came to an end before our enemies saw their defeat."

"Then how do you know?" Maki asked. "How are you talking to us at all?"

"I cannot explain it," Thijn shrugged the human vessel's small shoulders. "My energy became trapped between planes of existence. That is the only way I know how to explain it. My body died. My soul occasionally finds a way to cling to life. My people communicated telepathically. I have always believed that has something to do with my ability to cling to this world."

"You've done this before?" I asked.

"Not with this much success," Thijn said. "No one has been here in hundreds of years. I have never had the opportunity to converse with others before."

"Will you help us?" Alessa asked. "Can you show us how your people fought off the Gorgos?"

"The walls contain the answer," Thijn said.

"I don't understand," Maki said. "You mean these symbols?"

Thijn nodded.

"We can't read them. Are they in your language?"

"No, they are in the language of the ancients. My people were able to learn pieces of it because it formed the basis for all language in the galaxy."

"Why would such a species write symbols over your burials?" Maki asked.

"I do not know," Thijn replied. "Perhaps to mock us? To claim us even in death? Or maybe they possessed a conscience and buried us according to their customs. I do not know. I will never know for certain. I do know that these words gave my people the tools to eradicate our enemies."

"Can you read them for us?" I asked.

"I will do what I can. A light please?" Thijn gestured to the walls. Maki pulled out her flashlight and illuminated the lines of characters.

"What do you think about all this?" Alessa whispered to me.

"I don't know," I whispered back. "This Thijn character seems genuine, I suppose."

"I don't feel right about any of this. What about the human that body belongs to? Is she still in there somewhere?" she said.

"I hope so."

"Maybe Thijn can remain in her body long enough for us to save her," Alessa said hopefully. I didn't know how to respond to that. We'd both heard the Gorgos communicating through the human woman. From what I'd seen, it was already too late to save the human. With any luck, she was already long gone.

"This is the most important of the symbols," Thijn explained to Maki, who stood far too close for comfort. As I'd said, Thijn seemed genuine but if this was some sort of trap, we were all caught.

"What does it mean?" Maki pulled out her camera, ready to snap images.

"In your people's tongue, it literally means the light of sound," Thijn explained.

"That doesn't make any sense," Maki furrowed her brow. "Sound doesn't have light. Are you sure it's a literal translation?"

"I am," Thijn nodded. "These other symbols aid with context, though I am not sure how well they will translate into your language. This vessel's mind has been damaged. It is difficult to access her language center."

"Anything you can tell us is greatly appreciated," Maki said.

"Of course," Thijn nodded. "I-"

Thijn suddenly went very still. Unnaturally still.

"Thijn?" Maki said.

Tyehn reached for Maki and pulled her back a step.

The human's eyes shifted once more. They looked almost normal now.

"Help me!" Cried a feminine human voice.

Her eyes switched again.

"The ancient enemies are returning," Thijn's voice said. "Beware!"

The human's head started to shake rapidly back and forth. Something beneath her skin squirmed.

"Fools!" The voice of the Gorgo came through. "There is nothing you can do to stop us! We are eternal!"

The human opened her mouth wider than what should've been possible. Two distinct screams tore from her throat, one human and one that sounded like Thijn.

"We have to do something," Alessa pleaded. "We have to help her!"

"I don't think there's anything we can do," Axtin said. "We can't transport her like this."

"She's in pain!" Alessa cried.

The human, and whichever entity was currently possessing her, fell to the floor writhing and screaming in agony. She clawed at herself, shredding her own skin to ribbons.

"Make it stop!" She screamed. "Make it stop!"

"Do we have a sedative?" Alessa asked. "A stun gun? Anything?"

"We're all out," Axtin replied. "I never found the sedative from the med pack."

"Shit," Alessa swore.

The human lashed out at us. I couldn't tell if her goal was to harm us or to plead for help.

"We have to end it," I said.

"What?" Alessa looked up at me, wide-eyed. "You can't!"

"There isn't anything we can do for her except end her pain," I replied.

"Please!" The human wailed in multiple voices.

She dragged herself forward, latching onto Alessa's arm. She tried to pull Alessa down. If I hadn't been holding her, Alessa would've fallen to the floor along with the human.

"Axtin, take her."

Axtin walked over and whisked Alessa away.

"What are you going to do?" Alessa demanded.

"Don't look," I warned her but I knew she wasn't going to listen to me. I drew my weapon. The writhing human went still. She looked up at me with surprising clarity.

"Do it," she begged. "Before those horrible things take my mind away from me again. Please!"

"We can still save her," Alessa insisted. "She has control of her own mind right now."

"It won't last," the human said. "I can feel them pressing against my mind. It feels like a thousand snakes. End it!"

"Navat!" Alessa cried.

"End it!" The human screamed again.

I pulled out my weapon and fired a round into the human's chest. She fell backward and went still. I tucked my weapon away with a heavy sigh.

The human jerked. Her upper body launched upright into a sitting position.

"What the fuck?" I heard Maki gasp from the other side of the burial chamber. The human woman's eyes were milky white. She grinned even though her chest wound still bled violently.

"Thank you for making room for us," the voice of the Gorgo hissed.

I pulled my weapon out and fired a shot right between the human's eyes. She slumped over once more.

Now that her brain was destroyed, the Gorgo couldn't keep hold of her.

I watched something slither away beneath her skin and vanish, leaving only a corpse behind.

"It's over."

ALESSA

"What the fuck just happened?" was all I could make myself say.

I wiggled out of Axtin's grip, despite not being strong enough to stand without excruciating pain.

"I'm sorry," Navat said. From the mournful look in his eyes, I could tell he meant it. "I didn't see another option."

I wanted to argue. I wanted to insist that it didn't have to end this way but I knew that wasn't true. That poor woman. It must've been terrible to share her mind like that. It was amazing she held on for as long as she did.

"At least we learned something," Maki said in a shaky voice. "We learned that the Gorgos can still use a host so long as their brain is intact."

"That wouldn't have done them much good in this case," Axtin pointed out. "I didn't think they could use a dead host."

"They just did that to screw with our heads," Tyehn hissed. "It was a scare tactic."

"Well, it fucking worked," I sputtered.

"Come here," Navat said to me. "You shouldn't be putting any weight on your left side."

He stepped over the body so that I wouldn't have to. When he reached me, he lifted his arm so that I could situate myself at his side.

I wrapped an arm around his waist, hooking my fingers around his belt to keep myself upright. He placed his arm beneath mine, allowing me to use him for leverage to support myself.

"I'm sorry," he repeated.

"I know. I am too," I sighed heavily. "I just want to leave."

"We'll figure it out," he assured me. "There are only so many passageways and corridors we can take. It's only a matter of time before we're back on the surface."

"I hope you're right." I felt defeated. Seeing that woman go through what she went through in her final moments took a lot out of me.

"I know I am." Navat offered me an encouraging smile.

"What's our next step?" Tyehn asked. "Is this light of sound business worth looking into?"

"I think it is," Maki said. "Thijn said it was how the last inhabitants fought off the Gorgos."

"That means the Gorgos have targeted this place before," I said. "Why? What's so special about us?"

"The Puppet Master," Axtin said. "That must be what they're after."

"Then why go for humans as hosts?"

"I don't know," Axtin sighed. "I know as much as the rest of you do."

"I think the light of sound is worth looking into," I said.

"Agreed," Navat nodded. "However, I don't think we're going to solve that puzzle down here. We need to do some research."

"Maybe this old language is referenced in the archives somewhere," Maki said thoughtfully.

"If we're lucky," I agreed.

A pinging sound nearly made me jump out of my skin.

"What was that?" Axtin demanded, reaching for his hammer.

Another ping sounded off.

"Alessa, it's coming from you," Navat said. "I think it's your wrist unit."

"What?"

I lifted my wrist. Sure enough, my wrist unit was lit up and appeared to be working perfectly.

"But how?" Maki sputtered.

"The woman," I said with a start. "She grabbed me by this wrist right before she died."

"So?"

"Remember what Thijn said? His kind communicated through telepathy. Energy transfer! What if Thijn used that same energy to give my wrist unit a jump start?"

"Is that possible?" Tyehn asked.

"I don't know," I shrugged. "But my wrist unit is fully functional and I'm not going to waste another moment questioning it."

"Can you pull up the map?"

I tinkered with the wrist unit until the mini holographic projector popped up. A clear overhead scan of the map filled the little holograph screen. I released the breath I hadn't realized I was holding.

"Oh, thank goodness," Maki sighed.

"Come on," Navat jerked his head. "Let's get out of here."

Navat and I took our place up front, using the map to weave through the corridors in the direction of where we came in. Hopefully, the damage from the cave-in wasn't so terrible that we couldn't dig our way out.

We rounded a corner, heading into a pitch-black tunnel. I was trying to pick up the pace as much as possible, but Navat held me back.

"Don't push yourself," he pleaded. "We're getting out of here. Don't risk further injury."

"Easy for you to say," I scoffed.

"Believe me, it's not," he chuckled.

I was about to say something witty in return, but something thick and solid slammed into my stomach. Navat and I went flying backward. He twisted his body to protect me from the impact of landing.

He shone his flashlight into the darkness, illuminating the armored body of another spindly-legged creature.

"For fuck's sake," I muttered.

"Stay down," He urged as he climbed to his feet. He charged the creature. Tyehn and Axtin followed him.

"You don't have to tell me twice," I muttered. "I learned my lesson about those things. Watch out for the leg thorns."

I felt Maki's arms hook underneath mind. She pulled me back.

"Do you want to drive a knife into its gut this time?" I asked.

"I'll pass," she shuddered. "You're very nonchalant about this."

"Look," I sighed. "I've been beaten up, traumatized, and I think I technically died earlier. I don't have any more energy for anything other than putting one foot in front of the other and getting out of here."

"Understandable," Maki nodded.

"I have enough fear for the both of us," Bayla whispered in the darkness. I almost couldn't see her. She'd made herself tiny to cower behind Maki. Kip lurked behind her, watching the fight unfold.

Thankfully, the three alien men learned from last time. Axtin smashed at its legs with his hammer. Navat was able to get underneath it and empty his weapon into the tender space between armored plates. The creature gave a final shudder before collapsing dead on the floor.

"Well, now that wasn't too bad," Navat said as he helped me to my feet and tucked me under his arm. I took hold of his belt once more.

"Why do I feel like that was a final 'fuck you' from this place?" I muttered.

"It did feel that way, didn't it?" Axtin laughed from behind me.

I brought the map up once more. This time, Navat didn't fight me when I wanted to pick up the pace. I didn't care if it hurt more. I was done with this terrible tomb and the horrible monsters concealed within it.

"I say we blow this place sky high when we're finished researching," I said.

"You won't hear any complaints from me," Tyehn echoed.

"We should move the bodies from the burial altars before we do that," Maki said. "They were victims, too."

"Good point. I'll agree to that. Who knows? We might get another visit from Thijn if we save the bodies."

"Thijn was an energy mass, not a ghost," Maki laughed.

"What exactly is the difference?"

Maki's silence was the only answer I needed.

"Look, that's the chamber we came in from!" Axtin whooped. We spilled into the circular chamber. I squinted up at the harsh light pouring in from the skylight.

"Ready to dig us out?" I asked Navat.

"You have no idea how ready I am." He was all smiles as he set me down on a large slab of rock while everyone else went toward the caved in archway.

"We have to do this carefully," Maki warned. "The structural integrity was compromised when we came in. The last thing we want is for all this to come down on us."

I closed my eyes so I wouldn't have to look at the bodies littering the floor of the space. I only opened them again when I felt Navat's hand on my shoulder.

"Ready to go home?" He asked.

"You have no idea."

He scooped me up in his arms this time.

"It'll be faster this way," he explained when I gave him a strange look. I didn't argue. As we walked out of the final tunnel, I noticed a spot of blood on his arm.

"You're bleeding. I think one of those thorns snagged you," I said.

"You can patch me up in Axtin's shuttle if you like," he said. "You sort of owe me."

"Deal," I grinned.

Our group burst onto the surface with a series of victorious whoops. The sunlight felt so good on my skin. Tears pricked the backs of my eyes. I never thought I'd make it out of there alive.

After checking the camp for survivors, we wasted no time getting loaded up in Axtin's shuttle.

We were off the ground in minutes. No one was left. Either dead from the attack, or possessed, I didn't know.

"I can't wait to analyze these samples," Maki said.

"What samples?" Tyehn gave her a curious look.

"You didn't think I wouldn't take samples after being surrounded by so many specimens, did you?"

Maki opened her pack to reveal airtight samples of flesh, skin, and even hair.

"Please don't make me look at that," I winced.

"Sorry," she shot me an apologetic smile. "I just think we have a real chance at getting rid of the Gorgos now. I'm excited!"

"I'm excited for a hot shower," Kip said.

"I'm excited for a fresh bandage." Navat gave me a playful nudge.

"Of course," I grinned back. I pulled a med pack from beneath the seat and took out a roll of bandages.

As I changed Navat's bandages, I couldn't help but think about how much had changed since I went underground. I'd told my boss that I never wanted to work with a non-human team again, but after having my life saved by aliens at least a dozen times in the last twenty-four hours, I couldn't imagine not having aliens on my team.

"I'm glad you were down there with me," I told Navat.

His eyebrows shot up.

"Is that so?"

"I mean, you saved my ass more times than I can count," I shrugged.

"You saved mine right back."

"My point is, the five of us make a good team," I said.

"Are you saying you were wrong?" He gave me a wry smile.

"Yes," I rolled my eyes and smiled. "I was wrong."

"That's the most surprising thing I've heard since we started this mission."

"Oh, shut up."

NAVAT

The ride back to Nyhiem was blessedly quick. When we touched down on the roof of the building, dozens of personnel had come to greet us. I spotted General Rouhr in the crowd with a deep frown on his face.

Axtin landed the shuttle with ease. All of us eagerly spilled out, ready to greet our friends and colleagues.

"Give me a hand?" Alessa asked with a shy smile.

"Of course." I extended a hand to her and supported her while she climbed out of the shuttle. When she was close enough to me, I wrapped my arm around her waist and let her lean on me.

"I should get you registered as a service animal," she mused.

"A what?" I blurted.

"A special creature that helps people do daily tasks."

"Should I be flattered or insulted?"

"Depends on how you choose to look at it," I shrugged.

General Rouhr approached me.

"I'm expecting a lengthy report from you," he said.

"You'll get one, sir," I nodded.

"Your team gave us quite the scare," General Rouhr sighed. "We're glad to have you back in one piece."

He eyed my bandaged arm and Alessa's inability to put weight on her left side.

"Mostly one piece," he amended.

"That's why all of them, even the four humans, are coming to see me," Dr. Parr spoke up.

"I assure you, Evie, that's not necessary," I said.

"Oh? Is that so? Where's your doctorate? What medical course did you take?" Evie fired back.

"Battlefield medicine," I replied. "I'm fine. I assure you."

Evie scoffed and rolled her eyes.

"Oh, yes. The illustrious study of how to plug up wounds with whatever is lying around. Report to the med bay before I make you."

"Yes, ma'am," I chuckled.

Evie turned her gaze on Alessa.

"You too, please."

"Excuse me?" Alessa blurted.

"You've clearly sustained a significant injury," Evie said. "I'll need you to report to the med bay as well."

"No, thank you," Alessa smiled kindly. "I'd really just prefer to go home. It's been a hell of a day."

"You were injured on an assignment," Evie said. "That means you must go to the med bay until I give you a clean bill of health."

I bit back laughter at the exchange unfolding before me. I genuinely didn't know who was going to come out on top.

"I'm not under the employment of General Rouhr," Alessa replied. "I'd really prefer to go home."

"Actually, your company lent you out as a private contractor so, technically, for this assignment you do work for me," General Rouhr said.

"Exactly," Evie beamed. "To the med bay with the lot of you."

"But-" Alessa started to protest but I gave her a squeeze.

"Evie is the best and General Rouhr foots the bill," I whispered to her.

"Oh." Her eyebrows rose in surprise. "In that case, lead the way."

"I knew you'd come around," Evie grinned. "I like you."

Evie ushered us, as well as everyone else who came out of the tunnels, to the med bay.

"I don't have a scratch on me!" Axtin protested. "I need to get started on the pile of reports I'm going to have to fill out."

"Then I won't keep you long," Evie called over her shoulder.

"I'd like to call my family if that's all right," Bayla said.

"Absolutely," Evie smiled gently. "There's a comm unit in my office. It can call anywhere on the continent."

"Great. Thank you."

"How long do you think this will take?" Alessa whispered to me.

"Why? Are you that eager to get away from me?" I teased.

"No!" She said quickly, her cheeks turning a pretty shade of pink. "It's not that. I just want to take a shower in my own bathroom, change into my own clothes, and sleep in my own bed. Plus, I'm sure my family will want to see me. I usually contact them once a day."

"Your family is still alive?" I said.

"Yes." She gave me a curious look.

"I'm sorry," I said. "It's just that so many of the people we work with have lost at least one family member. It's not common to find someone like you."

"I know," she replied. "I'm incredibly lucky."

"I'm going to put you in that cot right there, dear," Evie said to Alessa.

"I'll go beside her," I volunteered.

"Are you giving bed assignments now, Navat?" Evie arched a brow.

"Only my own," I grinned back.

Evie rolled her eyes but allowed me to help Alessa into her cot. I plopped myself down on the one beside hers.

"You're probably going to be here the longest," I told her.

"Why?"

"You sustained a massive puncture wound by an unknown creature. Evie's going to want to study you."

"No," Alessa groaned and let her head fall back against the stiff pillow.

"And my patch up job likely wasn't up to scratch. Believe me, you want Evie to get in there and fix everything."

"Do you have to say it like that?" She laughed.

"No, but it's more fun if I do," I replied.

"For you or for me?"

"You, I hope."

"Are you always this nice after a life-threatening experience?" She asked.

"Absolutely not. This is a special occasion," I replied.

"Stop annoying my new patient." Evie appeared and gave me a gentle smack on my good shoulder.

"You're supposed to heal, not hurt."

"I can do both," Evie shrugged before taking a seat on a stool beside Alessa's cot. "What happened to you?"

"You'd better ask Navat," Alessa said. "I wasn't exactly conscious."

"Oh!" Evie's eyes widened with alarm. "Let me get you started on a brain scan, just in case."

Evie left Alessa's bedside and came back with a small chip with needle-like filaments protruding from its sides.

"You're going to feel a tiny pinch but there shouldn't be any pain after that."

Evie used the filaments to secure the chip to Alessa's temple. Alessa didn't even flinch.

"While we wait for that, tell me what happened, Navat."

I quickly told the tale of Alessa's clever thinking against the creature in the tunnels and the injuries she sustained.

"You patched her up on the floor of a tomb?" Evie shrieked.

"It's not like I had another option," I replied.

"Who knows what kind of nasty things got in that wound," she sighed. "I'm going to have to open you up and clean everything."

"Are you sure?" Alessa looked nervous. "I feel fine, all considered."

"I'm sure," Evie said. "What if there's an infection brewing inside of you? If the wound is closed, the infection could go into your blood. I don't think you want that, do you?"

"No," Alessa sighed. "But will it hurt?"

"Of course not," Evie grinned. "I have all the best sedatives and numbing agents."

"In that case, go to town," Alessa flipped her hand nonchalantly.

"I'm going to get everything set up and check on the other patients. I bet Axtin's already trying to sneak out."

"He just went out the front door," I said.

"Did he? Damn it, why didn't you tell me sooner?" Evie groaned.

"Entertainment, mostly," I grinned.

Evie rolled her eyes and marched after Axtin.

I looked over at Alessa, who was staring at the ceiling and clenching her blanket in a tight fist.

"Everything's going to be fine," I assured her. "Even if there are signs of infection, Evie will fix everything. She's sort of everyone's mother around here."

"I just want to sleep."

I noticed now how exhausted Alessa looked. She looked utterly drained.

"I know. You can sleep if you want to. You don't need to be awake for the brain scan."

"I don't think I can sleep after what I saw," she replied in a small voice.

"Evie can give you something for that too," he said. "Just about all of us take something to help us sleep."

"Really?" Alessa turned to look at me.

"Yes," I said. "You don't get to have a sound night's sleep after fighting an army of Xathi and their hybrids."

"That makes sense," she nodded. "But does it get better?"

"Over time, yes," I nodded. "The first few weeks are the roughest, though."

"Goody."

"Just remember that you're not alone."

Alessa's expression softened.

I'd been aware of her beauty since I'd met her, I just hadn't had much time to appreciate it between our little spats and fighting for our lives.

Now, I could appreciate it in full.

The one stolen kiss behind the tents hadn't satisfied my growing hunger for her.

Before I fully knew what I was doing, I got to my feet and crossed the small distance between my cot and hers.

I bent down and pressed a kiss into her forehead.

Most of the human women I knew seemed to like it when their mates did that.

Not that Alessa was my mate.

Of course not.

We were just running on adrenaline and terror.

A small thought niggled at the back of my head that I couldn't stamp out.

Could she be my mate?

"What was that for?" She smiled up at me.

"I suppose it's my way of thanking you," I scrambled to come up with a suitable answer. "You saved my life. You saved Maki's life. Bayla and Kip are alive because of you. Your map was the one that got us out of there. So, thank you."

"Thank you for not letting me die in there," she replied.

I opened my mouth to say something back but she reached up and grabbed the collar of my shirt. She pulled me down to her level, pressing her lips against mine.

I smiled against her mouth and kissed her deeper.

"Oh, for goodness' sake!" Evie tutted. Alessa and I sprang apart.

"Apologies," I grinned.

"No wonder her brain scan is going all wonky," Evie snapped. "I have to start it over again. Can you manage not to kiss her until it's done?"

"I can try," I winked.

"No promises," Alessa grinned back.

"I swear, I'm nothing more than a glorified babysitter," Evie groaned and restarted Alessa's brain scan. I couldn't stop smiling.

ALESSA

I decided to blame it on the trauma and the adrenaline. Why else would I grab Navat and kiss him like that?

Again.

Never mind that both times were the best kisses I'd ever had.

I wasn't in my right mind. We'd just spend a very stressful twenty-four hours together in a never-ending serious of life or death struggles.

Before that, I was giddy, celebrating finding the buried complex.

Of course, my brain was going to try to make all of that into something more than it was.

It was adrenaline.

And, perhaps, curiosity.

But I didn't expect him to kiss me on the forehead like that.

What was even more unexpected was the gentle warmth that flooded my body the moment his lips made contact with my skin. I wasn't prepared to feel that flutter in my chest, that quickening of my heart.

I wasn't the romantic type, not by a long shot. Sure, I always assumed I'd find someone and settle down but that always seemed like a long way off. I certainly never imagined I'd settle down with an alien. I wasn't about to start imagining that now.

Those kisses were a fluke.

It didn't matter how much I liked it. It didn't matter that I felt that fluttery feeling in my chest every time I glanced his way.

Evie was examining him now. I listened in as Navat tried to explain that his injuries were nothing.

"You do realize that you would've been patched up and out of here by now if you hadn't spent so much time arguing with me, right?" Evie folded her arms across her chest. "What is it with all you alien men and refusing to admit you need medical attention?"

"That's not true," Navat protested.

"The only times I haven't gotten lip from any of you is when you're completely unconscious when you're brought in," Evie said.

"I believe that," I spoke up.

"You're going to take her side?" Navat looked at me with mock horror. "After all I've done for you?"

"All you've done for her since she got here is mess up her brain scan," Evie tutted. "Which, should be finishing up any moment now."

Just like clockwork, the little device strapped to my temple beeped.

"Perfect," Evie grinned and gingerly removed the device from my face. "I'll go see what this says."

"Are you nervous?" Navat asked me when Evie was out of earshot.

"A little," I admitted. "I got knocked around a few times. Human brains are more delicate than they seem."

"I'm sure everything will be fine," he assured me as he swung his legs over his cot.

"What are you doing?" I asked him.

"Getting in trouble."

He came and sat down beside me.

"You're going to get yelled at again," I warned him. I wondered if he was going to try to kiss me again. Part of me wanted that so badly I ached for it. The other part of me wanted to shy away. I wasn't in the correct headspace to deal with big feelings like this. Hell, I didn't even know if my brain was working properly.

"Again, Navat?" Evie sighed when she returned.

"Do I need to be in my bed to receive a clean bill of

health?" He asked. "I just want to make sure Alessa is okay."

Evie's expression softened as she rolled her eyes.

"Fine, just don't get in my way."

She walked up to the other side of my cot and showed me her datapad.

"Everything looks good," she said. "You're lucky you didn't sustain any damage."

"I know," I replied. "My team took good care of me."

I peeked at Navat from the corner of my eye. He was smiling.

"Now, for the unpleasant part," Evie sucked in a breath.

"The part where you put needles in my temple wasn't the unpleasant part?" I asked.

"I need to cut open the new cell growth on your side and properly sanitize the wound," she explained. "I have numbing agents at the ready, but this isn't going to be fun."

"I thought you said it wasn't going to hurt," I frowned.

"It won't hurt but it won't be fun."

"Let's get this over with."

Navat took my hand and gave it a gentle squeeze.

"Do you want me here?" He asked. "I can leave if that would make you more comfortable."

I was tempted to say yes just so I would stop thinking about kissing him again.

"I'd actually like to have a familiar face around," I said. "Besides, I always seem to survive stuff when you're around."

"I do my best," he shrugged.

I laced my fingers through his and gave Evie a nod.

"First, the numbing agent." She picked up an unfortunately large needle and quickly injected the tender area around my puncture wound.

"Wow," I hissed through my teeth. "That was unpleasant."

"You can swear if you want to," Evie grinned. "You won't believe the string of curses I hear from General Rouhr's men."

"We're soldiers, not courtiers," Navat scoffed.

Evie shook her head.

"Can you still feel this?" She asked, rubbing my side.

"Not really."

"Great. I'm going to go ahead and start," she said. "You might want to look away. Even the bravest people don't always react well to watching themselves get cut open."

"Good call."

I turned to look at Navat. While I didn't feel any pain, I felt an unpleasant tugging sensation where I assumed Evie was slicing. I fought the urge to look.

"How about I distract you with some riveting conversation?" Navat offered.

"That sounds good," I agreed.

"Do you think you'll take another excavation job after this?"

"Fuck no," I laughed while trying not to move. "I'll never go underground again for as long as I live."

"I'm in agreement with you there," Navat said.

"Has Maki made it to the lab yet?"

"Nope!" Maki's voice rang out from farther down the room. "I'm still here."

"Glad to know you're doing all right," I called back.

"You like to tinker with things, right?" Navat said.

"I do," I nodded.

"I wonder if you could tinker with some of our lab equipment."

"I'm listening."

"Well, I'm not an expert on lab tech but I know we're going to be testing substances that we've never tested before. Maybe you could work with our lab ladies to make our machines more suited to our purposes."

"As long as they don't mind me working strictly with the hardware, I think that's a good idea."

"I'll talk to Leena when I get out of here," Navat said. "If I ever get out of here."

"I'm three fingers deep in your friend, at the moment. I apologize if that's an inconvenience for you."

Evie's peculiar choice of words made my cheek grow hot. It took all of my willpower not to glance down at Navat's fingers and give Evie's words an entirely new meaning.

Did numbing agents make people a little wonky in the head?

"Are you all right?" Navat asked.

"Never better. Why?" I replied.

"Because your cheeks have gone red," he said. "You're not running a fever are you?"

He placed the back of his hand over my forehead.

"Would you even be able to tell if a human was running hot?" I asked.

"No, but don't I get credit for trying?" He smirked.

"You're all clean and stitched," Evie said. "I'll put some regrowth serum on in a moment, but first we need to hook you up to a blood bag. You're low."

"That would make sense," I nodded.

"I'll grab you one."

Evie walked away. I took a peek at the new wound in my side. It was much neater than the old one. It hurt less too.

"I wonder what the recovery time for this is," I said.

"Not long once Evie gets that regrowth serum. Hers

is a proper serum and not something out of a spray canister," Navat chuckled.

"Thanks for staying with me," I said. "I feel like such a baby."

"You're allowed to want someone with you when your side is being cut open," Navat assured me.

I couldn't describe it, but something in his words spooked me. Yes, I was allowed to want him there. But should I want him at all? The more attached I got to him, the harder it would be to return to my normal life. I thought that was what I wanted but now I wasn't so sure.

I couldn't handle this right now. I needed time to sort out whether or not I really did have some kind of feelings for Navat or if this was a product of adrenaline.

"What's wrong?" Navat asked. "Are you in pain?"

"Yes," I nodded. "Would you mind fetching the doctor for me?"

"Of course," he nodded. "I'll be back shortly."

"Thanks."

Once he was out of sight, I breathed a sigh of relief. It would be so much easier to sort out my feelings when his handsome face wasn't in my line of sight. It was distracting.

I knew what I needed. I needed space to think.

Surely, these feelings would wear off once I put some distance between us. As nice as he is, I just couldn't handle intense emotions right now. I needed to clear my head. In order to do that, I needed to pull away from Navat.

It didn't help that I still wanted to kiss him.

Again.

NAVAT

I tossed and turned in my bed. In my mind's eye, all I saw was the thorn sticking out of Alessa's side. I did everything I could to shake the image away but it held fast.

This time, we didn't have enough supplies in the med pack.

Alessa bled out in my arms.

I sat up in bed. Light peeked in around the blinds. It was already morning. No point in trying to go back to sleep now.

For the past two nights, my mind tormented me with images of Alessa dying down in the tunnels. No matter how many times I told myself she was alive and well, I spent my nights fighting off those terrible images.

I hadn't heard anything from Alessa since I was discharged from the med bay. Since her injuries were far more severe than everyone else's, Evie wanted to keep her overnight for observation.

I didn't think too much of it. Alessa had been through a lot in the last few days. It made sense that she wanted time to herself.

The strange thing was, the more time I spent away from her the closer to her I wanted to be. I was still in shock that she kissed me so boldly.

There were several moments within the tunnels that I wanted to kiss her but held back. First of all, it wouldn't have been appropriate.

Second, I didn't want to share that moment with Axtin and Tyehn there to snicker over my shoulder.

The second day after we'd returned from our brush with death, General Rouhr called a meeting. I looked at the notification on my wrist unit. I saw Alessa's name on the required personnel list. Excitement sparked in my chest.

I hurried to the meeting room. More than anything, I wanted to see how she was doing.

I wasn't the first to arrive in the meeting room, but I'd arrived before Alessa.

"Hey," Maki jerked her head in my direction as a greeting.

"Hey," I replied and took the open seat next to her.

Tyehn sat on her other side. "How have you been?"

"I've spent the last two days resting," Maki said.

"How have you been sleeping?"

"Terribly," I admitted.

"Us too."

"Have you heard from Alessa?" I asked.

"I went to visit her this morning," Maki said. "She's doing really well. She barely even has a scar now. I think Evie was just about to discharge her."

Odd. I would've hoped she'd tell me she was being discharged.

"How is she doing otherwise?" I asked, choosing my words carefully.

"I think she really wants to go home," Maki replied. "She misses her family."

"I don't blame her. Hopefully, we can get her out of here soon."

"Is that what you want?" Maki gave me a knowing look. "I know strange bonds are formed when survival is at stake, but you two formed something different."

"Did we?" I arched my brow.

Make shook her head and laughed.

"Don't pretend you don't know what I'm talking about," she said. "There's something between the two of you. I know it."

She was right but I wasn't sure how comfortable I

was discussing my feelings for Alessa before I truly took the time to understand them.

"It might be a good idea to change the subject," Tyehn warned us softly.

Alessa walked into the meeting room. She swept the room with a cold gaze looking unimpressed. I expected her to take the open seat beside me but she took one on the opposite side of the room away from everyone. Though she looked healthier, she didn't look happy.

She looked pissed.

"Oh, my," Maki said under her breath.

I tried to catch Alessa's eye but she seemed to be doing everything in her power not to look in my direction. I didn't understand it. Hadn't she kissed me? Didn't that mean something to most humans?

"Are we ready to begin?" General Rouhr's voice tore my attention away from Alessa.

"Yes, sir." Maki stood up and took her place by the console at the front of the room. The pictures she took of the burial tombs lit up the display screen behind her.

"What's that?" Fen suddenly demanded. I twisted around to look at her. I hadn't realized she was here. It's rare for her to leave the *Aurora* nowadays.

"We found evidence of a society that lived here long before we did," Maki explained. "They were attacked by the Gorgos as well."

"Go back to the image of the writing," Fen requested.

Maki obliged.

"I know that script!" There was a delighted gleam in Fen's eyes. "It is the language of the Aeryx!"

"What are the Aeryx?" General Rouhr asked.

"They created the system that made space travel possible," Fen replied. She was so excited that she shook her speech pad whenever she spoke. "All of our ships, with the exception of human ships, are built off of their discovery."

"They lived here?"

"I was unaware that they had a settlement here," Fen said. "But that is most certainly their script."

"Can you read it?" Maki asked.

"No," Fen shook her head. "But my people have studied the language extensively. I will be able to dig up their research from our archives."

"We encountered what can only be described as a spirit inside the tunnels," Maki continued.

"You can't be serious," Vrehx rolled his eyes.

"I am," Maki nodded.

"It possessed the body of a young human woman," Alessa spoke up. "It called itself Thijn. Thijn started to translate some of the characters for us."

Maki pulled up the picture of the single translated symbol.

"We believe this symbol and the ones around it allude to how to defeat the Gorgos."

"If the Aeryx were able to successfully rid themselves of the Gorgos, they would've documented it. I'll get into the archives right away." Fen stood up and took her leave.

Alessa stood up as well. I thought she was going to speak more, but instead, she made her way toward the door. General Rouhr watched her with a concerned frown.

I stood up and went after her. No one tried to stop me.

"Alessa," I called after her as she walked quickly down the corridor. She didn't stop though she must've heard me. I jogged to keep up with her.

"What's the matter?" I asked her.

"Nothing," she said in a flat voice. "I just didn't see any reason for me to be there."

"General Rouhr wouldn't have called you in if he didn't think you were valuable," I replied.

Alessa rolled her eyes.

"I know exactly what the rest of you know," she said. "There is nothing I could tell him that Maki, or anyone else on the team, couldn't."

"The General never does anything without a good reason," I said. "I've worked with him long enough to know that."

"Well, I haven't," she snapped.

I grabbed her arm, forcing her to stop.

"Excuse me," she snapped and yanked her arm out of my grip. "What's your problem?"

Her tone alarmed me.

"I don't have a problem," I said calmly. "But I think you do."

"You're right." She offered a cold smile. "My problem is that no one will let me go home!"

"I'm certain there's a good reason for that," I assured her.

"Are you?" She narrowed her eyes.

"Yes. I've been doing this for a while now."

"That's terrific. Good for you." She tried to walk away again but I stopped her.

"Stop me again and I will get violent," she warned me.

"What did I do to warrant such hostility?" I demanded. "I've done nothing but try to help you."

"When did I ask for that?" She demanded.

"When you were bleeding out in the tunnels for starters," I pointed out.

"So that gives you the right to harass me?"

"I'm not trying to harass you," I snapped. My patience was wearing thin. "You kissed me, remember? Twice?"

She dropped her gaze.

"What does that have to do with anything?"

"I'm starting to think everything."

"Oh, please," she rolled her eyes. "It was just a stupid kiss. I was drugged out of my mind the second time."

"No, you weren't," I corrected her. "Evie hadn't given you anything yet."

"Whatever," she scoffed.

"Why are you fighting this so hard?" I demanded. "Is it because I'm an alien?"

"No," she said quickly. "It's not that! I know I was a jerk about the alien thing when we met, but I was wrong. I already told you that."

"Then what is it? There's something between us. You know it. I know it. Why are we dancing around it?"

"I'm not dancing around anything!"

"No, you're point blank avoiding it."

"You need to back off."

"Not until you tell me why you've shut me out," I said. "Don't I deserve to know why after everything we've been through?"

She looked at me with stormy eyes. Even now, I couldn't help but think about how beautiful she was.

"Don't try to emotionally blackmail me," she hissed. "I just need some time, okay? We've all been through a lot. I'm not sleeping. I can't keep my thoughts straight. I just need time."

"That's all you had to say," I said softly. "You should know by now that I have your best interest at heart."

The heated anger drained out of her expression. Now, she just looked exhausted.

"I need to go," she whispered. "I want to lie down."

"Okay," I nodded and took a step back from her so she knew I'd let her go.

"We'll talk, eventually," she said. "I just…"

She closed her eyes and shook her head.

"Need time," I finished. "It's okay. I'll be around."

She nodded, her gaze lingering on mine.

I was tempted to kiss her again, but before I could reach for her, she turned her back on me and walked away.

ALESSA

Tears welled in my eyes as I walked away from Navat. I wish I could make him understand how difficult this was for me.

It wasn't that he was an alien, it really wasn't.

Though, I was still struggling with the idea of falling for someone that wasn't human. How would that work? What if we had a family?

I stopped that train of thought before it could go any further.

I hated how easy it was for me to imagine a future with him, especially when a future wasn't guaranteed for any of us now that the Gorgos were here.

It wasn't until some time later that I realized that, in my anger, I'd walked the wrong way.

The med bay was on the other side of the complex.

Evie had checked me out, but I didn't have a room here or anything. I had nowhere else to go.

I walked back the way I came. From what I could tell, the meeting was over. I saw Maki and Tyehn leave. I hid behind a pillar until they were out of sight. I didn't want to talk to anyone else right now. I especially didn't want those certain, pitying looks I got when someone asks about my wellbeing.

"Miss Naro," a deep voice behind me startled me.

I spun around to find General Rouhr.

"Sir," I stammered.

"Are you well?" He inquired. "It's not usual for people to leave in the middle of a meeting."

"I found myself in need of some air," I said, which wasn't a total lie.

"Are you better now?" The concern in General Rouhr's eyes looked genuine.

"Not really," I answered honestly.

"That's understandable. You've been through a lot."

"I really just want to go home, sir," I pled.

"I know," he nodded. "I promise, I'll send you home as soon as I'm able."

"Why aren't you able now?" I asked. "Aren't you the one in charge here?"

"It's more than that," he said. "What you saw down there was valuable."

"I didn't see anything different than anyone else," I pointed out.

"I can see how you might think that. However, everyone experiences things differently. The more I know about the collective experience, the more I know about what happened down there. Your point of view matters even if you don't think it does."

There was something about him that extruded wisdom. I found that I couldn't argue with him.

"Yes, sir," I sighed with defeat.

"I'll get you out of here as soon as I can," he repeated. "Until then, I'll get a room sorted out for you. The least I can do is make sure you're comfortable."

"I'd appreciate that." I offered a smile.

"Someone will approach you with your room assignment soon," he said.

"Do I have to stay in the building until then?" I asked.

My question seemed to catch General Rouhr by surprise.

"No," he said after a moment of consideration. "Not at all. Feel free to walk around the city. Just, please, don't hop on the first shuttle out of here."

"That honestly hadn't occurred to me," I grinned.

"Good. It would be within my abilities to send someone after you and bring you back here," he said. "I don't want to do that do you."

"You won't have to," I assured him. "I'm going to get some fresh air. Thank you in advance for the room."

"Of course." General Rouhr dipped his head before striding away. I could see why his men respected him the way that they did. He seemed like a good leader.

I wasted no time getting out into the city. I'd been to Nyhiem before, but not recently. I was surprised to see how much had changed. The city streets were still scarred from the Puppet Master's vines, but there were tons of brand-new buildings nicer than anything we'd ever been able to build. It must've been a product of Mayor Vidia's housing relief program. I felt glad to see it flourishing.

I wasn't sure where I wanted to go. I didn't think that far ahead.

I wove through the streets for a while. I spotted an open market and walked through the stalls, looking at the food and wares for sale.

After a while, I grew hungry. I wasn't familiar with any of the restaurants here so I picked a random one on the same block as General Rouhr's compound.

I took a table in the corner. A smiling waitress bought a holographic menu to my table.

"The albeef stew is really good here," a woman's voice said.

I looked up to find a woman with a severe blonde bob and an intense gaze. Her sharp mouth was curved up into a smile. In a strange way, she reminded me of one of my strictest primary school teachers. As strict as that teacher was, she taught me more than any of the other's combined.

"Do I know you?" I asked.

"No, but it was only a matter of time before we're introduced. I saw you come in and figured I'd take the initiative. Do you mind if I sit?" She gestured to the empty seat opposite me.

Despite not knowing what was going on, I nodded.

"Thanks." She plopped herself down and offered me a hand, which I took. Her handshake was firm and a little painful. "Leena DeWitt. I work for General Rouhr. My lab is a few doors down from Evie's med bay."

"Oh," I said. "I think Navat mentioned the lab ladies once or twice."

"I'm one of the ladies. The main lady, if you will," Leena smiled proudly. "I hear you're a mechanical engineer."

"I am," I nodded. "Though, I was consulting on an excavation site for General Rouhr. That's how I got pulled into this mess."

"What happened to you and the team was terrifying," Leena said softly.

"You have no idea," I murmured.

"I have some idea. Axtin is my mate."

I blinked in surprise.

"Is he? He saved my life a few times. I was glad to have him there, though I don't suspect you feel the same."

"I do if he was able to make a difference," Leena replied.

"That hammer of his sure did," I chuckled. "I need to get one of those."

"He loves that hammer almost as much as he loves me," Leena chuckled. "Maybe even more so on certain days. I've been told I'm a bit of a hardass."

"You have to be in this world," I shrugged. "I've been called abrasive on more than one occasion, and that's just the nice way of putting it."

"So, you get it!" Leena tipped her head back and laughed.

"Are you one of the lab ladies who's working on reversing the Gorgo infection?" I asked.

"I'm trying to," Leena nodded. "Our data has been pretty inconclusive so far but Maki brought back a treasure trove of samples for us to pull apart. I'm optimistic."

"That's good to know," I said. "Getting those samples wasn't easy."

"I'm sorry for the team members you lost," Leena said.

"I'm still sorry that only two came out alive. I'd do anything to go back and change that."

"I know." She gave me an understanding look. "Believe me, all of us wish we could turn back the clock for some reason or another."

A lump rose in my throat.

"How long have you and Axtin been together?" I asked, desperate to change the subject.

"Almost two years, I think," Leena smiled. "It's hard to keep the timeline straight sometimes. So much has happened in such a short amount of time. Sometimes I feel like it's been fifty years. Sometimes it feels like the Xathi ship crashed down last week."

"I know what you mean," I nodded.

"Navat has been singing your praises to me since he was discharged from the med bay."

"Is that so?" I arched a brow.

"He thinks you'll be a real asset in the lab and that you could tweak the hardware of our machines," she said.

"I can give them a look," I nodded. "Especially if that means you'll be able to get more out of Maki's samples."

"That would be great. The hardware isn't my specialty," Leena said. "Navat seems taken with you."

"He's not," I said too quickly. Leena gave me a suspicious look.

"Look, I get it. Falling for someone of a different species is strange."

"Who said I was falling for him?"

"You blushed when I said his name. You're getting weirdly defensive about him. Do you think I was born yesterday?"

"We made a great team down in the tunnels," I said. "We saved each other's lives. We relied on each other. Adrenaline can make people feel things they wouldn't feel otherwise."

"You're partially correct. Adrenaline can enhance feelings but it can't create new ones out of thin air," she said.

"I never thought I'd be working alongside aliens let alone struggling with my feelings for one," I sighed.

"Ah, some honesty at last," Leena winked. "I know it's weird at first. It's hard to ignore the fact that they have green skin and super strength. But, surely, you've noticed that they aren't all that different from us on the inside."

"I suppose," I shrugged.

"You're not anti-alien, are you?" Leena gave me a stern look.

"No!" I snapped. "Sorry, I just get asked that a lot. I'm not anti-alien. However, I've noticed that destruction follows them. I gave the aliens a wide berth because I didn't want to get caught up in the danger."

"Destruction might follow them but they're rather good at dealing with it," Leena pointed out. "They're much better equipped than we are."

"I'll agree with that," I nodded.

"Can I get you any food?" The smiling waitress returned.

"Want to join me for lunch?" I asked Leena.

"Sounds great."

NAVAT

I still felt rattled from my conversation with Alessa. She looked so…unsure. Even when she was down in the tunnels surrounded by monstrous creatures and Gorgo infected humans she didn't look that unsure.

It was no wonder we were attracted to each other. Both of us would rather fight a rabid Gorgo than analyze our feelings.

Unfortunately for me, there was nothing to do but analyze right now. I was, essentially, on hold until Maki's samples were thoroughly tested and analyzed.

Even then, there wasn't a guarantee they would yield anything useful.

I sat at a table in the cafeteria with a tray of untouched food. I ran my last conversation with Alessa through my head over and over again, carefully turning over each word and sentence. I didn't know what to do.

Surely, there was a hint somewhere in her words.

What did she mean by needing space? Did she want me to ignore her from now on? Did she want a friend?

I was clueless and I hated this feeling.

"Do you have an issue with your food?" Axtin asked as he set his own tray down on the table and took the seat across from me.

"What?" I blinked in confusion.

"You're glaring at it like it murdered your family," he said.

"I'm just thinking."

"About Alessa?" Tyehn took the empty seat beside Axtin.

"Why would you assume that?" I asked.

"The only reason I ever give inanimate objects the death glare is when Leena's being particularly vexing," Axtin said.

"I'm thinking about the Gorgos, if you must know," I lied.

"Bullshit," Tyehn said. "You've been thinking about the Gorgos for weeks and never made a face like that."

"How closely do the two of you watch me?" I asked.

"I only watch you when you sleep," Axtin smirked.

"Yeah, I have daytime duty. Axtin got the better end of the deal," Tyehn joked.

"Oh, shut up," I chuckled. "You caught me. I was thinking about Alessa."

"I heard you two shared a sweet little moment in the med bay a few days ago," Axtin winked.

"She kissed me," I said, frowning at my tray of food.

"Try to contain your excitement," Tyehn said. "I thought you liked her?"

"When did I say that?"

"Come on," Tyehn rolled his eyes. "It's obvious there was something between the two of you in the tunnels."

"Maki said the same thing," I smirked.

"I'm quickly learning that Maki is never wrong," Tyehn laughed.

"I learned that after one day with Leena," Axtin said. "She never lets me forget it."

"Even when she's actually wrong?" I asked.

"That's the weird part," Axtin said. "I've literally never seen her be wrong about something. She's too smart for me. We both know it."

"That's not true," I said.

"Have you met Leena?" Axtin grinned. "She's brilliant. She's definitely smarter than me. It's amazing. She handles all the brainy stuff. I handle all of the things that can be solved with a hammer. We balance each other."

"When did you figure out that balance?" I asked.

"It took some time," Axtin nodded. "We didn't have a traditional start to our courtship."

"I think it's fair to say none of us have had traditional starts to our courtships," Tyehn jumped it. "We're on a foreign planet, for one thing."

"For another, random enemies are constantly invading. Hard to court properly in this kind of climate."

"Fair points," Axtin nodded. "The first step is to stop denying your feelings."

"Fine," I sighed. "I like Alessa."

"Good job," Axtin beamed. "Have you talked to her about liking her?"

"Not in so many words," I said. "I thought I was showing how much I care through my actions. I thought it was working. She was the one who kissed me in the med bay. She grabbed my shirt and pulled me to her."

"She clearly likes you too," Tyehn said. "So, what's the issue?"

"I must've done something wrong," I said. "She didn't speak to me for two days. She wouldn't even look at me during that meeting."

"You ran after her when she left. What happened?" Axtin asked.

"I wanted to make sure she's okay," I said. "She said she was fine, but she needed space."

"There's your answer," Tyehn shrugged. "Give her space."

"I can do that but I can't stop worrying about her."

"Is she a capable woman?" Axtin asked.

"Without a doubt."

"Is she a stable woman?"

"I think so."

"Then don't worry about her too much," Axtin said. "Tyehn, remember how strange it was to realize you were attracted to a human woman?"

"It was a little odd," Tyehn admitted. "It took me by surprise, to say the least."

"I imagine Leena had to take a moment to wrap her head around it as well," Axtin said. "Alessa could be struggling with that. Or she could be, you know, traumatized."

"Nothing takes away romance like a good dose of trauma," Tyehn added.

"Not helping," I sighed. "I'm trying to make the trauma of the tunnels easier for her to bear."

"You might not be able too," Tyehn said. "She's going to have to work through a good portion of it alone. She almost died down there. That's going to weigh on her for a while."

"It's either that or she's playing hard to get," Axtin shrugged.

"So, what do I do?"

"Be attentive without being overbearing."

"Wait for her to seek you out."

"Don't be pushy but don't be too distant either."

"Do something nice for her."

I placed my head in my hands and sighed.

"You do realize all of those little gems of advice were completely contradictory, right?"

"Welcome to the world of human women," Axtin grinned.

"You know what helps Maki when she's not feeling great?" Tyehn said. "Work."

"Work," I repeated.

"I'm not sure about that," Axtin said. "Ordinarily, I'd agree with the benefits of work on a shaken-up mind, but wasn't it her work that led her into the terrible situations?"

"Sort of," I said. "She doesn't do excavations often. Perhaps doing normal work tasks might make her feel better."

"Such as?"

I rubbed my chin.

"Alessa said she became a mechanical engineer because she loves making something from nothing," I said. "If I could give her an opportunity to do that, it might make a difference."

"What are you thinking?" Axtin asked.

"You know how I've been doing side work between missions?" I asked.

"Not really," Tyehn furrowed his brow. "What kind of side work."

"I wasn't aware of this either," Axtin said.

"Well," I cleared my throat. "It all started when Mayor Vidia broke ground on the new housing. There were tons of people who wanted to help but not a lot of them were qualified."

"But you are," Tyehn said.

"Exactly. My background is construction and I've been working with techniques and materials far superior to what the humans use here," I explained. "I started out giving classes down at their community center once a week. This was pre-Gorgo so I had the extra time."

"You just wanted to get out of patrol, didn't you?" Axtin grinned.

"Kind of," I smirked. "Once it became clear that once a week classes weren't enough, I started getting more hands-on. I used to have a rotation. I'd check-in at each site every day to make sure things were going the way they needed to. That's when I started noticing mistakes. My morning rotations turned into all day rotations. Before I knew it, I was spending whole days at a single site."

"Is that why you missed Evie's birthday?" Axtin asked.

"Yes," I frowned. I genuinely felt bad about that. I spent a week's wages on a gift for her to make up for it.

"How many of those new apartments did you build?"

"Practically all of them," I shrugged. "The materials the humans were working with were mostly bits of scrap. They would've never held together over time. I worked out a deal with Fen. General Rouhr helped with negotiations."

"That's all well and good, but how does this help you with Alessa?" Axtin asked.

"There's a new complex breaking ground soon. It's on the outskirts of town. It's meant to be a few blocks of apartments specifically designed for scientists. There's going to be a communal lab. It won't be as nice as the one we have here, but it's something."

"That sounds nice," Tyehn nodded.

"I think I should offer Alessa a position on the team," I said. "She could be my second in command."

"I have a feeling we're about to have our hands full with Gorgos," Axtin said.

"Exactly. Alessa could have a stable, non-Gorgo related job a stone's throw from here so we can protect her if she needs it. She could step in when I have to be here."

"Sounds like a perfect solution," Tyehn said.

"Do you think she'll go for it?" Axtin asked.

"I don't know," I shrugged. "I can't figure Alessa out. That's why I'm sitting here spilling my guts to you two over a pile of noodles."

"What if she doesn't like your plan?" Axtin asked.

"Will you stop it?" Tyehn drove his elbow into Axtin's side. "You're going to make him lose confidence."

"Navat has never had a problem with confidence," Axtin scoffed.

"That was before I met Alessa," I chuckled. "She could make me doubt whether or not I put my shoes on the right feet."

"You've got it bad, my friend," Axtin laughed.

"Don't I know it." I shook my head and returned my attention to my plate of now cold food. I felt good about my plan, I just hoped Alessa would feel the same way.

ALESSA

After my lunch with Leena, I spent a productive evening with her in the lab. I didn't make any modifications to her equipment but I could see where some would be beneficial.

Leena suggested drawing up a proposal containing my suggested modifications and submitting it General Rouhr. I was essentially stuck here until he decided he didn't need me anymore so I might as well do something useful.

The thought of having a worthwhile task to take my mind off of everything made me feel better.

General Rouhr secured a comfortable room for me within the complex. It didn't have a monitor or console, but Leena directed me to the business office filled with consoles anyone could use. She let me use her access codes since I didn't have one of my own. I stayed there working long after everyone else went to sleep.

The following morning, I felt better than I had in days.

From the moment I opened my eyes, all I could think about was Navat.

I shouldn't have been so short with him yesterday. He was trying to help me, despite the fact that he didn't have a clue as to what he was doing. I couldn't fault him for that, especially since I had no idea what I wanted to begin with.

Now that I felt like I had a purpose, I felt more balanced.

After grabbing a quick breakfast with Leena and some of the other women that frequently used the lab, I started asking around for Navat. I asked Maki first, but she hadn't seen him. She sent me to the training wing of the building. Most of the aliens started their days there.

I spotted Axtin right away. He was hard to miss. No one else had a giant hammer.

"Axtin!" I called out.

He looked over his shoulder and grinned.

"The lady of the hour! What can I do for you?"

"What do you mean by that?" I asked.

"I feel like at least eighty percent of my

conversations today have revolved around you," he smirked. "Leena's taken a shine to you."

"I've taken a shine to her. I just came from breakfast with her."

"Glad to know you're making friends."

"Who else has been talking about me besides Leena?" I asked.

"Who do you think?" Axtin smirked.

"Navat," I sighed. "Has he been telling everyone how awful I am? He'd be right to."

Axtin's brows shot up.

"No, not at all. He wants to help you. He just doesn't know what's wrong," Axtin said. "He thinks he's the problem."

"Crap," I groaned. There was my temper again.. "I snapped at him. I took my issues out on him. I want to apologize. Do you know where he is?"

"He mentioned going out to a construction project today," Axtin said. "I'm not sure which one. There are a few sites in the city ready to break ground."

"That's okay," I grinned. "I can figure out which one. Thanks, Axtin!" I was already jogging out of the training wing before he could say anything else. As I walked through the compound, I called my brother.

"Hey, Alessa. I haven't heard from you in a while. How are you?"

I wanted to cry at the sound of Garreth's familiar voice.

"It's been a crazy couple of days," I sighed. "I promise, I'll fill you in as soon as I'm allowed to."

"Allowed? What do you mean?" Garreth demanded. "Are you in trouble?"

"I was," I said. "But I'm out of trouble and I'm working with the people who helped me."

"I don't like the sound of that."

"I promise it's not as scary as it sounds," I assured him. "But that's not why I called. I need a favor?"

"What kind of favor?"

"Are you still managing that construction project in Sauma?"

"Yes. Why?"

"The company that hired you is based in Nyhiem, right?"

"Yeah, what's this about?"

"I'm looking for a friend who's working on a project here in the city. It's about to break ground but there are a few out there that fit that description. If I give you a name, can you tell me the site?"

"Sure thing," he said. "What's the name?"

"Navat. He's a Valorni."

"A Valorni? Since when do you have alien friends?"

"That's part of the long story I can't tell you yet," I replied. "Can you find him?"

"Give me a sec."

I heard a few taps and several beeps as Garreth scrolled through his wrist unit.

"Navat, you said?"

"That's right."

"He's assigned on the roster to be at the Oberon Hight Site. I'm sending you the coordinates now."

My wrist unit beeped.

"Perfect. Thanks so much."

"When are you going to stop by?" Garreth asked.

"Soon. I promise."

"Keep in touch," he said right before he disconnected.

I wasted no time getting to the Oberon Hight Site. It was nothing more than an empty, snow-covered lot. No one was there.

"Well, that was a waste," I sighed.

Not knowing what else to do, I started making my way back to General Rouhr's compound. Maybe Navat would be there. He might think it funny that I walked all this way to see him.

I decided to take the scenic route through the city. It was a crisp winter day. The piles of snow beside the streets sparkled under the white glint of the sun. I took a deep breath.

The air was so fresh, it reminded me of peppermint bark.

I approached a park. The center had been cleared out for an ice-skating rink. Friends, family, and lovers make their way around the rink in wobbly circles. Everyone was smiling and laughing.

I decided to sit on the bench and watch for a while.

"Alessa?"

I turned to see Navat walking toward me with a big smile on his face.

"Navat," I grinned. "What are you doing here?"

"I should ask you the same thing."

"I'm looking for you, actually," I admitted.

The smile vanished from his face.

"Is everything okay?"

"Yes," I said quickly. "Everything is fine! I just wanted to talk to you."

Navat appeared to visibly relax.

"About what?" He asked, taking a seat beside me on the bench.

"I want to apologize for snapping at you yesterday," I said. "It wasn't fair of me to lash out at you when you were just trying to help."

"It's okay," he said. "I know you're stressed out. I shouldn't have pushed you. You really came all the way out to my construction site to tell me that? How did you even know about it?"

"Axtin," I grinned. "And my brother works in

construction. He told me what project you're on. I didn't know you did this kind of stuff on the side."

"Yeah," he nodded. "General Rouhr and I agreed taking on side work was the best way to utilize my skills. I like the change of pace too. Being a soldier is exhausting sometimes."

"I can imagine," I nodded.

"Actually, I came out here this morning because I wanted to ask you something."

"Oh?" I raised my brows. "What?"

"I wanted to offer you a job."

Well, that wasn't what I was expecting.

"A job?" I repeated.

"That's right. I found your portfolio through your company. You're a talented mechanical engineer. I'd like to have someone like you on the team," he said.

That *really* wasn't what I was expecting.

"I already have a job," I blurted.

"I understand if you don't want to," Navat said. "But I figured I'd offer. You're the best candidate regardless of this past week's events."

"I appreciate that," I grinned.

"Want some hot cocoa?" He asked suddenly. "I heard it's popular with the humans."

"You've never tried it?" I gasped.

Navat shook his head.

"We're getting some, immediately!" I declared.

I pulled him up off the bench and dragged him to the nearest hot cocoa stand.

"Get it with marshmallows," I instructed. "It's even better that way."

"Two hot cocoas with marshmallows," Navat told a bemused cashier.

Hot drinks in hand, we made our way back to the bench. I watched Navat carefully as he took his first sip.

Somehow, for some reason, sharing this with him was important.

"I understand why humans like this," he nodded. "Your bodies can't tolerate extreme changes in temperature the way mine can. This would be perfect on a cold day."

"It is a cold day," I laughed.

"For you," he smirked.

"I changed my mind," I blurted.

"What?" Navat furrowed his brow.

"Tell me more," I said. "I'd like to hear more about the construction project and the details of the position you've offered."

"Really?" He smiled.

"Really."

"At this point, I'm willing to let you make the position exactly what you want it to be. I don't know how comparable the salary is, but you could potentially live within General Rouhr's building or get him to pay for an apartment."

"You think?"

I considered the idea of living here. Nyheim had grown on me, that was no lie. But I still liked working for my boss and with my crew.

It was a dilemma..

"You don't have to make that decision right now," Navat assured me. "We should work out the job particulars first."

"Is the Oberon Hight your only project?"

"No, I'm going to be running several at once. I'd be happy to bring you aboard all of them. We're working on a new community center. It's going to be state of the art if Fen will agree to let us in on Urai tech secrets."

"A community center," I said thoughtfully. "I like the sound of that."

"Nyhiem already has one but it's pretty run down," Navat continued. "I want the new one to be better in every way."

"It should have a garden," I said. "Even with all of Mayor Vidia's relief programs, some people are still short on food."

"That's a great idea," he smiled. "I want classrooms as well. General Rouhr and Vidia want to make our tech more accessible to the public, but we'll need to teach them how to use it."

Something about his unbridled passion for his projects stirred something within me. Before I knew what I was doing, I leaned forward and kissed him.

He kissed me back, but hesitantly.

"I promise I won't freak out and ignore you," I grinned.

"In that case, carry on."

Navat brought his hand up to cup my chin. He pulled me to his lips and kissed me until our hot cocoa turned cold.

This time I didn't back away, this time I didn't let the doubts and fears in my head distract me.

I wanted this.

I wanted him.

"Alessa," he groaned, breaking away for breath as I nestled into his chest. "I need to ask you..."

"Anything," I murmured, lips against the hot skin at the base of his neck. "Anything you want."

Too fast, too fast! all my doubts shrieked in chorus.

"Want to look at some schematics for a building with me?"

I smiled, breathing deep, letting all my fears subside.

Navat was perfect. He'd always understand me, never rush me, even when I couldn't say the words.

"I thought you'd never ask."

NAVAT

I woke up with a sharp pain in my neck. I opened my eyes to see an unfamiliar room. It was clean and utilitarian.

I realized I was in one of the rooms in the compound.

"Good morning," Alessa's voice chimed from somewhere behind me. I carefully craned my neck. I was sitting on the floor.

Had I slept here?

The last thing I remembered was sitting at the desk inside this room working on ideas for the community center with Alessa.

"What happened?" I grumbled.

"We were working but you fell asleep," she answered. I twisted around to see her. Apparently, I'd slept on the floor with my back pressed against the side of her bed.

I don't recommend it.

She was sitting cross-legged on her bed flipping through a datapad. She was wearing different clothing. Her hair was wet.

"How long have you been up?" I asked.

"About two hours," she replied. "I tried to wake you but you sleep like a rock. I tried to wake you last night too but once you were out you were out."

"I'm a heavy sleeper," I admitted. "How hard did you try to wake me?"

"I shouted," Alessa giggled. "And I shook you a few times. No reaction."

"That sounds about right." I stretched and groaned. "What have you been doing while I slept?"

"I kept working on plans," she grinned proudly. "Want to see?"

"Absolutely." I was going to climb up onto her bed but she shimmied down and sat on the floor beside me before I could get up.

"Look!" She was practically wiggling with excitement. "I drew up plans for a tech center. It's set up for hands on learning classes. Nothing would be too complicated to install, in theory. And look at this!"

She flipped to a schematic that looked like a roof design.

"It's a charity kitchen," she declared. "We could get culinary students to work it for college credit. The food could feed families that haven't recovered from the Xathi invasion, the Puppet Master's attacks, or the Gorgo madness."

"That's brilliant," I smiled. "This is all brilliant."

She was brilliant. My brilliant, beautiful mate.

Without thinking, I leaned over and pressed a kiss into her temple. She leaned into me with a blissful smile on her face.

"You're in a good mood," I teased.

"I feel good," she replied. "Working makes me feel good. Being around you makes me feel good."

"That's quite the revelation. What brought this on?"

"You know how I said I needed space to think?" She said.

I nodded.

"Well, it turns out I needed space to not think," she said. "I was overthinking everything. I was listening too intently to my thoughts and not enough to my other senses, like my feelings. My feelings tell me that I care for you. Simple as that."

Her words shocked me. I knew how I felt, but I didn't want to rush her.

I'd been prepared to wait, for as long as it took, for her to come to terms with her own emotions.

I wasn't prepared for this at all.

"I care for you, too," I said. "I care for you a great deal more than I ever expected to care for anyone."

"I'm sorry for disrupting your expectations," she grinned and leaned in for a proper kiss. I held her against me and I savored the sweet taste of her mouth. My tongue teased her lips. She opened her mouth, allowing full access.

White hot lust tore through my body. I'd been ignoring the physical effects she had on me since the day I met her.

I had a job to do.

Lives were at risk. I couldn't allow myself to be distracted by her perfect body and stormy eyes.

Now, there were no more distractions.

I didn't have to talk myself out of my attraction to her.

She moved so that she sat in my lap with one leg on either side of me.

"I can't believe I was so deep in denial," she sighed against my mouth.

I wrapped my arms around her waist and pulled her tight against me.

"I'm glad you've pulled yourself out of it," I replied.

She wore a light jacket over her tank top. I pulled it down, revealing her golden shoulders and toned arms. I kissed down her neck and across her clavicle. She tipped her head back and let out a sigh that was pure music to my ears.

Removing her jacket wasn't enough. I needed to see more of her, taste more of her. As if she read my mind, she lifted her arms. With great care, I removed her thin tank top. She wasn't wearing anything underneath.

After discarding her tank top, I caressed her perfect breasts. I stroked my thumb over her stiffening nipples, eliciting gasps and moans of pleasure from her. Her moans only furthered my arousal. I pushed my hips up against the apex of her thighs, allowing her to feel how hard she made me.

"Oh," she sighed as I ground against her, the scent of her pleasure flooding the room spurring me on.

She reached down, pressing her hand against my hardened length. Without hesitation, she undid the clasps of my pants and freed me from their confines. Her stormy eyes grew wide as she took in my size.

For a moment I was worried. She was so small. What if I hurt her? What if-

"This is going to be fun," she whispered, licking her lips.

If possible, I got harder.

She pushed herself back so that she sat on my shins and bent down. She took my entire length in her mouth. I reached underneath her and played with her breasts as she sucked me. As if they had a mind of their own, my hips rocked into her mouth.

I grasped her head gently, holding her still while I pushed myself down her throat. She looked up at me with those thunder cloud eyes.

They twinkled with delight and mischief. With one hand and some strategic wiggling, she pushed the remainder of her clothing off.

I almost reached my climax when I saw her place her hand between her thighs.

Instead, I pulled myself out of her mouth and brought her closer to me.

"I need to feel you," I murmured to her.

"I'm ready." Her voice was nothing more than a breathy whisper. I held her around the waist and lifted her up. Slowly, never looking away from her captivating gaze, I lowered her onto me. Her whole body shuddered as I entered her.

I started off slow, reveling in her tightness, still concerned about our mismatched sizes, but Alessa was way ahead of me.

She took control, setting the pace as she ground against me. She gripped the sheets of the bed behind me, using them for leverage to move her slender body faster and faster.

My pleasure was building quickly as she worked herself further down my straining cock.

I leaned forward, taking one of her breasts in my mouth and swirling my tongue over her nipple.

"Yes," she sighed, egging me on. Since she didn't need my help staying upright, I moved my other hand between her legs, stroking her clit while she rode me.

Within moments, her entire body seized up. She trembled from head to toe, gripping me tightly as she threw her head back. I grabbed her lower back, realizing she was no longer able to balance herself. Watching her reach her climax sent me over the edge.

I pressed my lips to her neck and shuddered against her warm skin as I emptied myself into her.

For a while, neither of us could move.

I was the one who regained the ability of speech first.

"I had a surprise planned for you today, you know?" I murmured into her ear.

"A bigger surprise than this?" She looked down at our naked bodies and winked.

"Not quite," I chuckled. "This makes my surprise rather underwhelming."

"Tell me anyway!" She giggled.

"Have you ever been to the scrapyard?" I ask.

"No, but I know of it. I've heard it's gotten quite full this year."

"It has. General Rouhr and everyone under his

command has clearance to enter the scrapyard. That includes you now."

Alessa's eyes lit up.

"Do you want to poke around and see if you can find some nothings to make a functional something?" I asked.

"Absolutely!" She beamed. "However, I think I need to take another shower."

"Mind if I join you?" I winked.

"Only if you promise to do things to me that would make General Rouhr regret giving me this room," she grinned.

I nearly choked as the meaning of her words settled.

"You should not think more often," I said as I helped her to her feet.

"Fear is what kept me from realizing my feelings sooner," she said as we walked into the bathroom. "It took me way too long to realize how stupid that was."

She turned on the water and stepped in. I followed her.

"I mean, seriously! I spent twenty-four hours certain I would die. What's more terrifying than that? Accepting my feelings for you shouldn't have been as scary as it was," she said.

"The mind works in strange ways," I said. "That's something we all have in common, regardless of species."

"Such wisdom," she smirked at me.

"I'm looking forward to sprinkling you with my gems of wisdom from here on out," I grinned back.

"I'm looking forward to getting to know you outside of a life-threatening situation." She looped her arms around my waist and held her body against mine as I stiffened again.

"That's sound great." I lifted her up so that I could kiss her sweet lips, and she wrapped her legs around my waist.

"Remember, we live on Ankou," she said. "So, the non-life-threatening situations will end before the week is over."

"I suspect chaos is in the forecast."

"When is it not?"

"But before it get here," I growled darkly, slowly lowering her slick folds onto my swollen cock, taking a dark delight as the pleasure took her over, "There's something else in your future."

I drove into her, again and again, as the orgasm washed over her, sweeping me along with her.

No matter what the future held, she would be mine.

My mate.

ALESSA

Navat and I spent most of the following week in bed. He had an apartment in Nyhiem but often stayed with me since I had the room at my disposal.

We got strange, but approving looks, everywhere we went within the compound.

"I didn't realize so many people were invested in our relationship," I whispered to him as we walked hand in hand in the direction of the cafeteria.

"You have no idea," he murmured back. "Everyone's been waiting for us to stop dancing around it. Especially Tyehn, Maki, and Axtin."

"It's not my fault I had to work through some emotional damage," I joked.

"I hope you don't blame yourself for anything," Navat said, his tone soft but serious.

"I sort of do," I shrugged. "I was the one so adamantly in denial about everything. I tried to write off my feelings for you as a product of adrenaline."

"To be fair, we'd both had a high hit of adrenaline last week," Navat shrugged.

"Don't defend me." I playfully nudged him. "I take full responsibility as the asshole in this situation."

"You're clearly forgetting what an asshole I was to you."

"Okay, fine," she sucked in her cheeks. "You and I are both two assholes who prefer life-threatening situations over dealing with our scary feelings. Fair?"

"That's fair. I'm happy to be an asshole with you any day."

"If Tyehn, Maki, and Axtin were expecting a gooey, romantic fairytale we should probably apologize to them upfront," I joked.

"That's a good idea," Navat agreed. "They're meeting us for breakfast. I'm excited to take in their reaction."

"Me too," I grinned.

Together, we walked into the cafeteria. Maki, Tyehn, Axtin, and Leena were already seated. All of them looked delighted to see us holding hands.

"What do we have here?" Axtin teased. "Did I have too much to drink last night or am I really seeing what I'm seeing."

"Your eyes are correct." Navat pulled out a chair for me.

"When did this happen?" Maki asked me. She and Leena stared at me, their eyes glittering with interest.

"About a week ago," I replied.

I winked at Navat as he walked to the serving line to get food for both of us.

"And you didn't say anything?" Maki gasped.

"I wanted to wait until the right moment," I shrugged. "Besides, Navat and I have had a busy week."

"Oh, I'm sure," Leena winked.

"No, seriously," I laughed. "We've been designing features for a new community center on the other side of town."

"Is that so?" Maki asked. "How exciting. You'll have to show us!"

"I will once I iron out some of the kinks," I assured her.

"I'm sure you're talking about kinks other than the ones in your plans," Leena said under her breath.

"Damn right I am," I grinned.

Maki and Leena slapped their hands over their mouths to stifle their giggles.

"What are you three laughing at?" Tyehn demanded.

"Don't worry about it," I waved him off.

Navat returned with two trays of food. As soon as

he took his seat, all three alien men received alerts on their comm units.

"General Rouhr's calling a meeting," Axtin sighed.

"Just for the strike teams?" Leena asked.

"It looks like he wants everyone from the expedition to go in," Navat said.

A knot tightened in my stomach. That still happened whenever I thought about our time in the tunnel. I'd almost convinced myself that I wouldn't have to think about that time again. Navat must've sensed my nerves. He reached under the table and squeezed my leg.

"It must be important," Maki said as she wiped her mouth and pushed up from the table. "Let's go."

"If you want to sit this one out, General Rouhr will understand," Navat whispered to me.

"No," I shook my head sharply. "It's okay. I can handle this."

There was hesitation in Navat's eyes.

"I'll be okay, I swear."

"All right," Navat nodded. He extended his hand to me and we followed Maki and Tyehn out of the cafeteria with Axtin trailing behind us.

We entered the same meeting room we were in the week before. The Urai, Fen, stood beside General Rouhr and spoke to him in hushed, robotic tones from her speech pad. A beautiful blonde woman next to a scarred Skotan tapped her fingers on a datapad, looking worried.

Navat and I sat side by side, fingers laced together.

"Are you okay?" Navat asked.

"Yeah," I nodded. "I just think it's weird that I'm still here. I'm not contributing any new information."

"You're part of the team now," Navat smirked. "That means you get to sit through all the boring meetings."

"Goodie," I giggled.

"Are we ready to begin?" General Rouhr asked.

"Yes, sir," Navat said.

"Great. Fen, I give you the floor."

The Urai recalibrated her speed pad to a higher volume before she started speaking.

"I've been able to successfully translate the writing on the walls within the burial chambers."

My heart quickened.

"What does it say?" I blurted.

"It is centered around a specific phrase," Fen said.

"The light of sound?" Maki asked.

"Precisely." Fen's galaxy colored eyes reflected surprise.

"That was the only symbol we knew the meaning of," she said.

"Right," Fen nodded. "The symbols around that one

lead me to believe 'sound' is the most prominent word in that phrase, rather than 'light.'"

"But what does it mean?"

"This symbol here," Fen pulled up a zoomed in image of one of the glyphs. "It means birth or first. It changes the meaning of the word 'light'. In this case, light metaphorically means beginning in the same way sunrise means the birth of the day."

"The beginning of sound?" Navat asked.

"The first sound, more accurately," Fen said.

"Thijn said the key to defeating the Gorgoxians was in that phrase," Maki said, brow furrowed. "What is the first sound?"

"That required more complex research," Fen explained. "A literal translation wasn't good enough. I had to look into the lore of the Aeryx to fully understand the potential meaning of the words."

"How accurate is your interpretation?" Tyehn asked.

"Since I cannot check it against an original source, meaning an Aeryx, I have to assume there's some error," Fen said. "However, it's all we have."

"Go on," I urged her. I was on the edge of my seat now. If that wall really did contain the secret to defeating the Gorgo's, I wanted to know.

"These symbols here," Fen pulled up more close-ups. "Reference a gate. Looking through their lore, I believe those symbols mean a metaphysical gate. A gate to the mind. It's a gate that can be opened and shut. Putting the first sound within the mind gate will push the Gorgo out."

"That doesn't make any sense," Axtin shook his head.

"Maybe we misunderstood Thijn," Maki said. "Maybe Thijn was confused."

"Maybe it wasn't Thijn at all," Navat suggests. "It could've easily been a clever Gorgo trying to trick us."

"But then why would they give up a key piece of the puzzle?" Tyehn wondered.

"Unless the symbols don't mean anything at all,' Maki sighed. "They were found in a burial chamber. What if they're nothing more than a prayer or something similar? What if the meaning is purely sentimental?"

"I think we've hit another dead end," Navat sighed.

"Wait," I said. "Let me think for a moment."

"What is it, Alessa?" Navat asked but I waved him off. I grasped a trail of thought in my mind, trying to follow it to a logical conclusion. It was on the tip of my tongue. I had all the pieces I needed. I simply needed to make sense of them.

"If I were to write a public message about how to kill someone, do you think I would write plainly?" I asked. "Do you think I'd write 'I'm going to kill Maki' on a monitor and leave it for everyone to see?"

"Hey!" Maki grumbled.

"No, I don't suppose so," Navat said.

"So why would the Aeryx do the same? If the Gorgos knew instructions to kill them were written somewhere, wouldn't they have destroyed them?"

"That's what I would do," Axtin said.

"What if the mind gate means memories?" I asked. "Remembering something is like opening a gate inside your mind, right?"

"Go on," General Rouhr encouraged.

I swallowed hard, realizing how many eyes were on me.

"What if the beginning of sound is something that triggers a memory?" I proposed. "Think about it. The Gorgo's infect minds. They take away the identity of the host. Sure, an identity is in facial features and mannerisms but true identity is in life-shaping memories. If Gorgo's can somehow block that, they could eradicate and identify from the inside out."

"But how could they do that?" Maki asked.

"I don't know," I shook my head. "But what if the beginning of sound is something that triggers an identity solidifying memory?"

"I'm not sure I follow," Navat looked at me with a furrowed brow. I took a deep breath.

"Years ago, my brother was severely injured in the woods. He screamed. That scream is burned in my brain. When he screamed, I learned several hard lessons about the world that shaped me into who I am now. If the memory that contained those lessons was gone, I'd be a different person."

"So, you're saying sounds can trigger memories blocked by the Gorgos?" The blonde woman said slowly.

"It sounds ridiculous, I know. But it's the only thing I can think of that makes sense," I said.

"I like that interpretation," Fen said. "It fits the literal translations and works with the Aeryx lore."

"I'm willing to dedicate resources to looking into that theory," General Rouhr said. "Sibyl," he glanced at the blonde woman next to the scarred Skotan. "Would you be willing to put your resources against this angle as well?"

She smiled, and for an instant I saw a horrible grief in her eyes. "Of course. It's what I'm here for."

"Brilliant, Alessa." Navat squeezed my hand.

I looked at him. I couldn't make myself smile. I was too worried.

"What if I'm wrong?" I asked.

"Then we go back to the drawing board until we're right," Navat said. "We're going to figure this out. I promise."

I thought about the sad looking woman. What had she seen? Who had she lost?

And the Skotan standing with her. Whatever happened, you could tell they'd face it together.

I gripped Navat's fingers tighter.

Together.

NAVAT

I piloted out of the jungle in a one-person aerial unit. I'd been at the dig site for three days. A new excavation team had started work after the last meeting with General Rouhr.

They'd been assigned to comb through every inch of the tunnels and tombs to find something that supported or disproved Alessa's interpretation of the symbols in the burial chamber.

They were also looking for the rest of the possessed humans.

The first day I arrived, the mission was to recover all of the bodies we had no choice but to leave behind. Unfortunately, nature had taken its toll on then.

There wasn't much left for testing and we had to

inform all of the families that an open-casket funeral wasn't going to be an option.

That was the worst part.

Actually, that wasn't true.

The worst part was how none of the families were surprised when they received the news. Did they grieve? Absolutely. But there was no shock in their voices when we informed them of their kin's fate. People disappearing and turning up dead was becoming entirely too common here. Hope was slowly being squeezed out of the planet.

I was determined to stop that from happening.

Once the bodies were removed, the studies began. The new excavation team was hand-selected by Maki and Alessa, though neither of them had returned to the site. I didn't blame them. I didn't want to come back either, but I wasn't given the choice. General Rouhr wanted the solders who were most familiar with the area to help break in the new ones.

After this, I hoped to never return unless it was an emergency.

The Puppet Master agreed to take an active role in the site's security, which was deeply appreciated.

The few combat-trained Urai offered to help as well. I was glad to have their advanced weapons protecting the new excavation team.

The one-person aerial unit was convenient but

frustratingly slow. It took me nearly four hours to reach Nyhiem and I had to stop and change out the fuel cells twice. I wasn't going to travel this way again, that was for damn sure.

All I wanted to do was get back home and see Alessa.

After our last meeting with General Rouhr, she was allowed to return to Sauma. She stayed for a few days but quickly came back. She was invested in the community center project as well as the community lab. When she wasn't doing that, she was working on updating Leena's lab equipment. Yesterday, she alluded to another secret project. I was excited to see what that was.

In such a short time, Alessa had become a whole new person. Rather, she was the person she always was. I had to frequently remind myself that I met her in a time of deep stress, that I was still getting to know the real Alessa. I adored everything I knew and I felt certain I'd adore everything I was to learn.

I also knew, without a doubt, that she felt the same way about me.

She was openly affectionate and sweeter than sugar made from flower nectar. I hated being away from her these past three days.

When I landed the aerial unit, I leaped from it before the engine finished powering down. I ran down three flights of stairs, taking the steps four or five at a time until I reached the lab floor.

I burst through the lab doors without warning. Leena nearly jumped out of her skin then looked like she wanted to murder me.

"You can't just burst in here like that! What if I'd been holding something flammable? Or acidic?" She snapped.

"I'm sorry," I raised my hands in surrender. "I'm looking for Alessa."

"She's in the workshop."

Leena jerked her head toward a spacious closet that, up until recently, had been used for storage. Now, it was converted into a makeshift workshop for Alessa to tinker in. She was able to make as much noise as she needed without running the risk of disturbing any of the lab ladies.

I knocked on the workshop door.

"Oh, you'll knock on that door but you can't be bothered to knock on the main one?" Leena hissed.

"I'm sorry," I said through laughter. "I promise to knock next time."

"You better." Leena returned to her work with a huff.

Alessa opened the workshop door. Her face was smudged with grease.

Her stormy eyes lit up when she saw me.

"Navat!" She shrieked and jumped into my arms. I didn't care that she was getting grease and oil all over my clothing.

I kissed her hard.

"Can you two please get out of sight before you do that?" Leena complained.

"Sorry!" We both said in unison.

I carried Alessa into the workshop just as Leena muttered something about how thankful she was the workshop was soundproof.

"I didn't think you'd be back until tomorrow morning," Alessa grinned.

"I plowed through my work today so I could get back early."

"How's the site?" Some of the joy left her eyes when she mentioned the dig site.

"Terrible," I shuddered. "It's in bad shape. I think something tore through there to get at the bodies."

Her face went a shade paler.

"I'm sorry," I sighed. "I shouldn't have said that."

"No, it's okay," Alessa shook her head. "We should be able to talk about it without feeling sick to our stomachs."

"That might take a while," I admitted. "Being there made my skin crawl."

"At least you can go back there," Alessa said. "The

thought of going there makes me feel like I can't breathe."

"You'll never have to go back there if you don't want to," I assured her. "No matter what anyone tells you."

"Thanks," she nodded.

We stood in silence for a moment before her eyes lit up again.

"I finished moving into the new place earlier today," she grinned.

Now that she didn't have to remain on the premises, General Rouhr allocated an apartment between here and the construction sites for her.

Coincidentally, it was in the same complex as mine.

"How do you like it?" I asked.

"It has more windows than yours," she teased. "But your unit has the better bathroom."

"I care about bathrooms more than I care about windows," I shrugged.

"Good because I'm not trading." She stuck her tongue out at me.

"I hope you won't mind if I drop by for dinner every night," I said.

"Are you kidding? I insist upon it."

I bent down to kiss her, finally feeling like I was home. And later, maybe I could convince her that maybe she didn't care about windows that much.

Or convince General Rhour's housing director that we really needed a double.

"Are you going to tell me about that secret project?" I murmured against her mouth.

"Maybe," she whispered against my lips. "You're terribly distracting, do you know that?'

"Me? Never."

I backed her up until her back was pressed against the cool, white wall of the workshop. She looked up at me, breathless and wanting. I was about to devour her when something caught my eye.

"What's that?" I asked.

There's a huge humanoid looking hunk of metal in the corner of the workshop.

"That's the surprise," she grinned. "It's going to be a suit. I'm basing it around my measurements, so you won't fit inside."

"A suit?" I repeated.

"That's right. It essentially takes every tool needed at the construction site and turns it into an extension of your body," Alessa explained. "No more searching for tools. It also can bear a considerable amount of weight so heavy lifting will be considerably safer."

"That's incredible! Have you tested it yet?"

"Not yet. There are still some kinks to work out. The prototype should be finished in about two weeks," she guessed.

"It's going to revolutionize the business, that's for sure."

"And, hopefully, cut down on building time."

"Absolutely brilliant," I beamed down at her.

"You say that a lot about me," she smirked. "I'm beginning to think you're buttering me up for something."

"Or I simply adore you, have you considered that?"

She made a big show of pondering my words.

"No, that can't be it. I think you're up to something," she teased.

"Is that right?" I pulled her back to me and kissed her hard. Her breath caught in her throat as I left a trail of kisses down her neck. "What do you think I'm up to?"

"I don't know," she whispered in my ear as she slipped her hands beneath my shirt. "But I plan on taking a long, long time to find out."

"Take all the time you need," I replied. "I'll be here."

"Forever?" She arched a brow.

"Forever and a day, if you like."

"Sounds like a good deal to me."

The pressure is on for our heroes and heroines. They have a clue that might help them in the fight against the Gorgos, but can they decipher it in time?

And will the price of the final battle be too high to pay?

Coming up next?

The final book in the Conquered World Saga...

She's his best friend. While the war rages around them, that's all she can be.

Or is it?

With the war against a deadly enemy coming to a head, K'ver scientist Sa'lok lives for the moments

he's assigned to work with human pilot Teisha.

She's smart, funny and level headed. Nothing would make him risk their friendship.

But when their closest ally is betrayed, she's thrown into unimaginable danger.

And his reaction to Teisha's peril isn't just wanting to protect his friend.

It's the rage that comes with a threat to his mate.

Teisha loves three things: her sister, her sister's kids, and speed.

After her promising career in linguistics was destroyed in the Xathi attacks, she became a pilot, helping the Alliance forces however she could.

Well, there might be another thing.

Person.

Sa'lok.

This just isn't the time. And he probably doesn't like her that way. Not like that.

And the end of it all can they win the battle, but still lose their hearts?

Keep reading for a sneak peak!

XOXO,

Elin

PLEASE DON'T FORGET TO LEAVE A REVIEW!

Readers rely on your opinions, and your review can help others decide on what books they read. Make sure your opinion is heard and leave a review where you purchased this book!

Don't miss a new release! You can sign up for release alerts at both Amazon and Bookbub:
bookbub.com/authors/elin-wyn
amazon.com/author/elinwyn

For a free short story, opportunities for advance review copies, release news and the occasional cat picture, please join the newsletter!
https://elinwynbooks.com/newsletter-signup/

And don't forget the Facebook group, where I post sneak peeks of chapters and covers!

https://www.facebook.com/groups/ElinWyn/

SA'LOK: SNEAK PEEK

T eisha

"Pull it toward you," I said, raising my voice so that I could be heard over the growl of the hovercraft's twin engines.

Sitting between my legs, Lyrie shifted her weight nervously and reached toward the yoke with her tiny hands.

I laid my hands on top of hers and, being as gentle as I could, I pulled the yoke toward us. The hovercraft's nose pointed up almost immediately, and the engines pushed us away from the ground and toward the bright blue skies overhead.

"Higher, higher," Lyle squealed from behind me, and I let a smile spread across my lips as I obliged.

Tilting the yoke toward me, I used my free hand to flick a couple of switches on the panel and redirected some extra power to the engines.

Their growl turned into a furious roar, the hovercraft's fuselage rattling and shaking, but neither of the kids showed any fear. If anything, it was the opposite.

The twins were just seven, but they were already as passionate about flying as I was.

Syra, their mother, wasn't exactly happy about it—no mother really enjoys having their children too far away, especially if too far away means being in a metallic box hundreds of feet up in the air—but she trusted me with the kids all the same.

And she was right to do it.

As their aunt, I would never do anything that would put really them in harm's way. I loved them more than I did myself.

But that was life on Ankou.

Risk and reward. They'd have to learn a little bit of the danger soon enough.

"It's all you now," I said as I pushed on the yoke and stabilized the hovercraft. Slowly, I removed my hands from Lyrie's and let her have the controls.

She nodded quietly, an expression of absolute focus washing over her face, and she held the yoke tightly as the hovercraft zoomed through the vastness of the blue sky.

"Bring us back around," I continued. "Tilt it a bit left."

Doing as she was told, Lyrie banked the ship left and settled in a circular trajectory over the woods. Once she straightened the ship, I looked back over my shoulder to ensure Lyle was enjoying himself.

I didn't need to worry.

He had both his hands on the cockpit window, forehead pressed tight against it, and he was looking at the sights with pure fascination.

"Say hi to your mother," I laughed, pointing down at the small outpost right underneath us.

A tall wooden palisade encircled a group of squat buildings, one main road cutting through the outpost from one end to the other; it couldn't even be called a village, but it was home all the same.

"Where?"

"There," I replied, pointing at the tiny figure standing in front of one of the houses.

It was hard to make out who that figure was from a distance, but I had absolutely no doubt it was Syra. Judging by the time, she was probably hanging the laundry to dry on the clothesline I had set up outside our house.

"Hi, mommy," the twins cried out at the same time, and I had to grab the yoke as Lyrie let go of it to wave at her mother.

Smiling, I reached for the panel and turned one of the engines off, allowing the air resistance to slow the hovercraft down.

Giving a quick glance at all the numbers and metrics on the dashboard—I've always relied more on instinct than on my technical expertise—I started to make a controlled descent, the belly of the hovercraft almost grazing the outpost's wooden palisade as I made a beeline toward our house.

"Already?" Lyle asked, his words thick with disappointment.

"Yeah," I laughed. "You have to do your homework, remember? Your mother will kill me if I keep you away from the books for too long. We'll fly some more tomorrow, alright?"

Carefully, I lowered the hovercraft onto the extension of overgrown grass that separated the house from the shed where I kept the hovercraft whenever I was away.

The clothes hanging outside swayed aggressively as I landed but, thankfully, they held onto the line.

I really, really didn't want to have to redo the washing, and that'd be my fate if the gusts from the hovercraft knocked them down.

"Off you go, kids."

"Homework! Right now," Syra cried out from the doorway, as if to punctuate what I had just said. She wore an apron over a pair of blue jeans and a faded black t-shirt, but her youthful appearance was betrayed by the stern look on her face.

Her eyes shone in the same way our mother's eyes had whenever she wanted to make it clear we were to obey immediately.

I couldn't help but smile at the memory, despite the twinge of sadness.

The twins jumped out from the hovercraft once I opened the doors, and they marched dutifully inside the house, barely sparing their mother a glance as they went.

I was checking the hovercraft's panel when I noticed Syra walking toward me.

Placing both her hands on the ship's nose, she gave me a thin lipped smile, her brown eyes shooting daggers at me through a few locks of her blonde hair.

"I thought we had talked about it," she finally said with a sigh.

"Talked about what?"

"The kids," she replied. "Homework before playing. You know."

"C'mon," I laughed, poking my head out of the

window just so I could look at her. "Remember when we were kids? Did we ever follow any rule like that?"

"Yeah, well, just wait until you're a mother. That devil may care attitude will bite you in the ass."

"Look at you, acting like such a grownup," I teased her.

Popping the pilot's door open, I climbed down from the hovercraft and made my way toward her.

She was still looking at me with a stern expression, but she mellowed out once I kissed her forehead.

Even though she was two years younger than me, Syra had always been the responsible one, and she hated whenever I treated her as if she was the oldest of the two.

It didn't help that I looked younger than I really was.

"I'm serious, Teisha," she sighed. "Life's tough as it is. I just want them to have a shot at a good life."

"I know you do." Laying one hand on her shoulder, I gave it a gentle squeeze and smiled. "And they'll turn out just fine. These two are some of the brightest kids I've ever come across. And they're brave, too."

"Thank you," she merely said, and this time it was her turn to kiss my forehead. Without saying another word more, she turned on her heels and walked back inside the house.

I stood there, leaning against the hovercraft, and

watched her go as the sun started its descent past the horizon line, a bright shade of orange spilling across the sky.

Syra was right—after the war, life had become tough. She had lost her husband during the fight against the Xathi, and was left to raise two children by herself.

Always keeping her chin up, she fought tooth and nail for the twins to have a happy life.

Even though I didn't worry as much as she did, I could see where she was coming from. I just hoped I was helping more than I stressed her out.

After her husband died, I moved in with her so I could help, but I wasn't really sure about how successful I had been.

There were times I wasn't around much, always flying on behalf of the Alliance League and General Rhour, and that meant the burden of raising the twins fell on her shoulders alone.

Sure, the money helped, but it only went so far. I was a part of a human pilot auxiliary program, and that meant I was on auxiliary wages.

Sometimes I couldn't help but wonder if it wouldn't be better for me to be around the house more often.

I had a degree in linguistics and anthropology—an interest that took the backseat once I got my first taste of the open skies—but even if the pay would have been higher, there weren't a lot of university jobs open right now.

Maybe in a few years we'd all be back on our feet, and I could get something that brought in more money, while allowing me to be home every night to help Syra with the kids.

Someday.

"Come in, Teisha," a voice crackled through my comm unit, derailing my train of thought. *"Are you there?"*

Recognizing that voice as belonging to my favorite K'ver, I smiled as I picked up the small communication device I had hanging from my belt.

"I'm here," I said. "What's up, Sa'lok?"

"Are you free?"

That was Sa'lok.

He never tiptoed around a subject, and he always cut straight to the chase. Most of the aliens were like that, especially the K'ver, but Sa'lok's background as an engineer really defined him as a straight-shooter.

A man that was always looking for solutions instead of dwelling on problems.

I liked that.

"Yeah, I'm free," I replied, immediately forgetting all about my plans of having an office job in the city. "Do you need a pilot?"

"*I do. I need someone to fly me to Glymna.*"

"What's there?" I asked him. Glyna wasn't exactly a hub of activity for the General's men, at least the last time I checked.

A small city carved into the earth, it was more like a relic of the first colonists attempts at urbanization than a proper modern city.

"Don't tell me you're going on vacation," I teased. "There are much better places to visit, you know?"

"*And how would you know that?*" He threw right back at me, his tone one of amusement. "*I don't remember you ever taking a day off.*"

Then, before I could say something, he continued, more serious now. "*There's been a development against the Gorgo, and I've been asked to consult. The Puppet Master is helping as well, and Glymna's one of the easiest points of access for him.*"

"Sounds good to me. Where are you?"

"*Nyhiem,*" he replied. "*Can you pick me up in an hour?*"

Smiling, I looked at my hovercraft.

It wasn't exactly a pretty model—its maker had filed for bankruptcy even before the war, and its outdated lines were too angular and stern—but I knew every single component hiding under the fuselage.

I had restored and retooled the entire thing myself, after all.

"An hour?" I laughed. "Please, I'll be there in thirty minutes."

"Won't you need to pack a bag?"

"Nope." I always kept a go-bag in the cargo hold, one with everything I needed for at least a week, and that meant I was always ready to go in a minute's notice.

Unlike those pilots that liked taking their time with preparations, I preferred to be ready all the time.

"Then see you soon, Teisha."

Sa'lok

"Stand clear!"

Folding my arms over my chest, I did as I was told and took a couple of steps back as the flight marshal, a spindly human guy in an orange vest, waved his two light sticks and directed Teisha's hovercraft toward the landing pad.

Even though the bright hangar lights bounced off her windshield, I could still see her leaning over the ship's controls, her petite figure and honey-blonde hair enough to make me smile.

"You're late," I told her the moment she climbed down from the hovercraft, her hair cascading down her shoulders in soft waves.

Quickly, she closed the distance between the two of us and punched my arm playfully.

"The kids didn't want me to come," she shot back as an explanation. "But I'm not late. It took me twenty-five minutes to get here. You're the one who arrived early. Seems like someone missed me, huh?"

"Why would I be missing you?" I laughed, cocking one eyebrow up as I grinned. "If I wanted to have someone around to bust my balls all the time, I would have already told the General I want to work with Vrehx."

She pursed her lips and gave me an annoyed look,

one that just made me laugh even more. "Come here, you," I told her as I took one step forward and wrapped my arms around her. She did the same happily, resting her head against my chest. "How are the kids?"

"They're growing up fast," she whispered. Against my K'ver frame, she seemed even smaller in comparison. Fragile, even. "You should come meet them."

"I'll see if I can ask for a day off once I'm done with Glymna. Your sister, how is she doing?"

"She's fine," she replied, but I could tell by her tone of voice that she wasn't telling me the whole truth.

Not that I was surprised. Syra was still mourning her husband while raising two kids. Never an easy situation to be in.

"Now, what's up with this Glymna business?"

"You heard about the new site one of our archaeologists uncovered?"

"I heard a thing or two," she admitted with a small shrug. "But I don't know much about it."

"And you've heard about the new possessions, haven't you?"

"The Gorgoxians, right? Everyone's talking about it."

"Yes, the Gorgo," I nodded, using the shorthand name the teams had been using for the possessed. Or the non-corporeal entities who had possessed the poor human hosts. Once the infection had taken place, there really didn't seem to be much difference.

"Apparently some of them were trying to dig a hole right in the middle of the Sika jungle. There was an underground structure there, it turns out. Some sort of holding structure built by an ancient race called the Aeryx. They used it to house those who had been infected by the Gorgoxians."

"So, a prison?"

"Not exactly," I continued. "More like a hospital. I know the General called for a big meeting a couple of days ago, and they figured out that the Aeryx had discovered a way to get rid of the Gorgo. A cure, if you will. Thing is, everything we've managed to get from the structure is in a language we don't recognize. Our Urai friends say that it can be translated but—"

"You need linguists."

"That's right."

"So did you call me here as a pilot or as linguist?"

"Well, I do need to get to Glymna," I smiled. "But you're proficient with languages, and that might come handy. We'll see how things go. A lab has been set up in Glymna, the best site for the job and the Puppet Master, and we'll be working out of there on a solution."

"Alright, this is an interesting job, I'll give you that much," she said, returning my smile as she tucked a lock of her hair over one ear.

"But why are you consulting with the guys in there? You're not exactly an expert on ancient civilizations or dead languages. Why do they need a chemical engineer, and one that's an expert in biological weapons to boot?"

Rek. I'd been dreading that question, but I hadn't been able to get through to the General's office yet.

I should have started the process before contacting her. No one should ever fly that fast, especially not a fragile human.

"I can't answer that right now."

I knew that my answer would infuriate her—more than anyone I knew, Teisha hated unanswered questions—but this time I wasn't teasing her or fooling around.

What I had to do in Glymna was classified, General's orders.

I was pretty sure I'd be able to get Teisha the needed clearance, but I still needed the General's authorization for it, and for that, I needed my comm to get through. "You're going to have to wait."

Her eyes narrowed, then she shrugged.

"In that case, let's get going."

She might be annoyed, but she'd deal with it. Teisha knew how the military worked as well as any soldier.

Grabbing my bag from the ground, she pressed it against my chest and quickly spun around. I watched her climb into the hovercraft, her movements liquid and smooth, and found myself shaking my head.

Why was she always in such a hurry?

"C'mon, what are you waiting for? You keep standing around like that and we're gonna die of old age before reaching Glymna."

Once inside Teisha's ship, I waited until the doors were closed to fasten my seatbelt, and then fired up my own panel and helped her check if we were ready for takeoff.

Five minutes later and we were leaving Nyhiem behind, the brightly lit streets of the city like a sprawling cobweb underneath us. Ahead of us there was nothing but darkness and the clear sky, thousands of shining stars strewn across the nightly canvas.

Sitting behind Teisha, and fully knowing that she couldn't see what I was doing on my screen, I quickly fired up a message to the General and asked for Teisha to be granted the necessary clearance for a prolonged stay on Glymna.

The approval came through ten minutes later.

I hadn't doubted it would, not for a moment.

One of the toughest pilots in the auxiliary pilot program she had been handpicked by the General as one of the pilots working directly under his orders.

To become one of the General's fliers was an honor

few humans had received, and she was the first human woman to get it.

Smart, brave, and talented, she had been an asset for the government ever since the Xathi decided to wreak havoc.

More than just that, she was also the best company someone like me could have. No matter how dire the situation was, Teisha always kept her head up, and she always had a witty remark on the tip of her tongue.

Whenever she was around, my job became more...fun.

Our friendship was an unlikely one, all with the anti-alien sentiment going around, but it also felt like the most natural thing to happen.

"You're quiet back there," she called over her shoulder. "You know how nervous that makes me."

"Just considering if I can integrate with your craft from here," I teased. "I'm not sure if my implants can handle something this antiquated."

"Jerk. My baby is a think of beauty."

I couldn't see her face, but I'd bet a week's pay she'd stuck her tongue out.

Together, we just clicked. Of course, all that just meant I was being constantly harassed by the rest of the guys on my team.

Much like the humans, they had a hard time believing two persons from different genders could become such close friends without anything *interesting* happening.

I didn't pay them much heed.

She was an attractive young woman, no doubt about that, but as much as I liked having her around, I was always so busy that I just didn't have the time to wonder about those things.

Much.

"Up ahead," Teisha finally spoke up after a couple of hours. Looking from behind her and over her shoulder, I saw bright lights coming straight up from the ground a couple of miles ahead.

"They're signaling us." Without waiting for me to say something, she lowered the power on the engines and dove straight toward the lights.

Only when we were closer did I manage to get a good look of the city.

Unlike most of the cities in the planet, Glymna seemed to grow down instead of up. The place was similar to a gigantic meteor's crater, with the city occupying its inside.

The various districts were like water drops slowly dripping down the inside curvature of a glass.

It was hard not to marvel at the way the monstrous rocky slopes were covered with buildings and streets that had been carved straight into the rock.

Cramped stairs zigzagged through the residential

districts, their inclination something that would give pause to those afraid of heights, and there were large openings here and there that seemed to lead into underground tunnels.

No wonder the Puppet Master had wanted us to set up shop here.

"Take us to Hangar C," I told Teisha as I checked my notes. "It's the closest one to the lab, and they're already waiting for us there."

She took us there fast, diving straight into the crater and making their way toward the large metallic structure that jutted out from the rock, right near the end of the slope.

"What do I do now?" She asked me as we landed, turning on her seat so that she could look at me. "Wait for you here? Or should I go looking for a hotel to stay in?"

"You're not going to be waiting here," I laughed, already grabbing my bag and opening the hovercraft's door.

Climbing down from the ship, I held one hand out to Teisha. "You're coming with me to the lab."

"I thought you said whatever you're working on was classified."

"It is," I smiled. "But the General gave you clearance on the way over. I was waiting for it, but you swung by too early."

"Does that mean—"

"Yes," I said. "You'll be working with me on this."

"Now you're talking." Jumping out from the cockpit with renewed energy, she offered me a wide grin and then followed me out of the landing platform.

A governmental aide was already at hand to help us, and we followed him out of the hangar and into a maze of underground corridors that led into a sealed vault door.

"Your biometrics have already been inserted into the system," the aide said in a bureaucratic tone, pointing at the panel mounted to the side of the door.

Nodding, I went toward the panel and let it scan my fingerprint and retina.

Immediately, the door hissed as the hydraulics system came alive and forced it to swing back on its reinforced hinges.

Stepping through the doorway, I glanced back to ensure Teisha was following after me, and then waited as the door closed again, leaving the aide behind. Ahead of us was an expansive corridor, the walls made of floor-to-ceiling glass panels that offered us a 360 view of the various lab rooms.

To our side was the room where a translation team was working on translating the Aeryx languages, and a couple of steps ahead was what seemed like a chemist's lab, all of it packed with state-of-the-art tech.

"This is impressive," Teisha whispered, looking around with a kid's sense of wonder and fascination.

"This is the nerve center when it comes to the Gorgo," I explained. "The General and other staff are the ones pulling the strings, but when it comes to the real action it's all happening here. Have you met Mariella?"

"Nope," she answered as we stopped next to a human woman who was poring over some text on a computer. She turned to face us and smiled.

"It's amazing what you were able to do with decrypting alien languages," Teisha said. "I've read about some of your work on the 'net. I'm excited to be working with you!"

"Thank you," Mariella said. "I left my notes open on this network to share with you. But I'm actually off to see the General about another problem." She laughed, swept her hair back into a quick braid. "It's never just one thing at a time anymore, is it?"

We bid her farewell as she hurried away.

"Alright," Teisha nodded quietly, skimming over the files and transferring them to a tablet for reference. "Where are we at?"

"The Urai have managed to translate some of the runes we found in the dig site," I continued, turning toward the translation laboratory to watch as the various translators—humans and Urai—worked around a massive table, a large and old-fashioned blackboard mounted against one of the walls.

In it, all manners of runes and possible translations had been drawn up in chalk. "We're in the early stages of the process, but we believe that whatever the Aeryx used had to do with memory."

"Memory? What does that mean?"

"To be honest, I'm not sure," I shrugged. "All I know is that I've been asked to start working on an antidote for the Gorgo infestation. I plan to start with the chemical processes that relate to memory in humans, and then go from there."

"That's like looking for a needle in a haystack."

"Why would you be looking for a needle there?" I asked her, right before I realized that it had to be one of those human sayings. "Anyway, you're right. It's not an easy task. But with the Puppet Master's help, maybe we'll get somewhere."

"Well, at least we have a plan," she muttered under her breath. Then, turning around, she looked straight at me. "Now, how bad is this Gorgo infestation? I've been hearing a lot of rumors, but no one really seems to know what's happening."

"Honestly?" Pursing my lips, I hesitated before replying.

In the end, though, I gave it to her straight. More than anyone in my life, she deserved to know the truth.

But still, my stomach knotted.

"It's bad, Teisha. Really bad."

GET SA'LOK NOW!

https://elinwynbooks.com/conquered-world-alien-romance/

DON'T MISS THE STAR BREED!

Given: Star Breed Book One

When a renegade thief and a genetically enhanced mercenary collide, space gets a whole lot hotter!

Thief Kara Shimsi has learned three lessons well - keep her head down, her fingers light, and her tithes to the syndicate paid on time.

But now a failed heist has earned her a death sentence - a one-way ticket to the toxic Waste outside the dome. Her only chance is a deal with the syndicate's most ruthless enforcer, a wolfish mountain of genetically-modified muscle named Davien.

The thought makes her body tingle with dread-or is it heat?

Mercenary Davien has one focus: do whatever is necessary to get the credits to get off this backwater mining colony and back into space. The last thing he wants is a smart-mouthed thief - even if she does have the clue he needs to hunt down whoever attacked the floating lab he and his created brothers called home.

Caring is a liability. Desire is a commodity. And love could get you killed.

https://elinwynbooks.com/star-breed/

ABOUT THE AUTHOR

I love old movies – *To Catch a Thief*, *Notorious*, *All About Eve* — and anything with Katherine Hepburn in it. Clever, elegant people doing clever, elegant things.

I'm a hopeless romantic.

And I love science fiction and the promise of space.

So it makes perfect sense to me to try to merge all of those loves into a new science fiction world, where dashing heroes and lovely ladies have adventures, get into trouble, and find their true love in the stars!